The poem "Love Without Hope" on page 260 is taken from *Collected Poems*, 1965, by Robert Graves and quoted by permission of the author.

Away to the West

RUTH TOMALIN

ISIS
LARGE PRINT
Oxford

First published in Great Britain 1972
by
Faber & Faber Limited

Published in Large Print 2008 by ISIS Publishing Ltd.,
7 Centremead, Osney Mead, Oxford OX2 0ES
by arrangement with
the Author

British Library Cataloguing in Publication Data
Tomalin, Ruth
    Away to the west. – Large print ed.
    1. Large type books
    I. Title
    823.9'14 [F]

ISBN 978–0–7531–8030–3 (hb)
ISBN 978–0–7531–8031–0 (pb)

Printed and bound in Great Britain by
T. J. International Ltd., Padstow, Cornwall

CONTENTS

A brown wood vole
digging beneath goosegrass and weasel nettle
tossed out the matchless fragments chink by chink,
bright as a bracken frond, a kingcup petal,
moss, or a beetle's back, a firecrest feather —
motes of a Roman pavement, link by link,
that once beat down the forest: left to sink
into the mines of the returning mole
under the goosegrass roots and growing weather.

The badger's halls
threading the white pavilions of the downs
followed through hewn ravines and furrowed ways
the hilltop battlements of older towns:
the circling storms, the little winds that stole
to mew in crevices, the valley haze
and drifting rains of immemorial days
saw the mosaic derelict, the walls
outlived again by nettle, brock and vole.

I

ALL ROUND THE MOON

CHAPTER
ONE

When the front door snapped shut behind Lily, leaving her alone in the flat, Rowan stood on her hands to celebrate her freedom; then flipped back to her feet and darted to the sitting-room window. Through green sprays of lemon bushes on the balcony, she watched Lily scuttle away down the sun-white pavement towards the King's Road. Gone to meet her Daniel. Hours of freedom lay ahead.

Rowan listened to the silence, indoors and out. The flat was empty, the square was empty. It was Whit Saturday. Everyone but herself was out and away. The long afternoon stretched before her to carry out her test. This was what she had hoped for, but had not dared to count on.

This afternoon, she and Lily were supposed to be together at Kew. Her mother was visiting friends, and had at first proposed to take Rowan with her. Seeing the look of dismay on her daughter's face, she had exclaimed quite sharply, "Don't look like that!"

Rowan opened her mouth to ask "How?", then shut it again without speaking, her eyes on her mother's frown. They were at breakfast. The whole Saturday hung in the balance.

"Flabbergasted," said Father. But Mother would not smile. Rowan waited, thinking — It's because I went back to Ireland for Easter. Mother's started worrying again, in case I like it best there, in case we're "out of touch". She was familiar with this post-war anxiety of mothers; all her friends had suffered from it, coming back two years ago from the country. Returning fathers, like her own, were more concerned in case their children might be out of hand. By now most parents were safely over all this, but Rowan's mother was having a relapse. She said after a moment's silence, "I'm sure Grandmother takes you out with her sometimes?"

"She doesn't. She always leaves me at home — at the farm, I mean. I have tea in the office with Grandfather, we have toasted cheese and bantams' eggs, as many as we like." She stopped, aware that she might have made things worse. Father murmured, "There. Trump that."

"Don't, Hal."

Yes, don't, pleaded Rowan silently. Was the afternoon to be wasted in Wimbledon? No; her mother said with resignation, "Well! You'd rather stay with Lily, then? You could have a picnic at Kew, and see the bluebells."

Rowan let her face light up. She made no attempt to explain that a picnic should have some object — to pick cowslips for wine or blackberries for jam; to paint, with her Aunt Lizard; even to hunt for four-leaved clovers out in the country with Father, while he watched village cricket. Looking at bluebells was not enough; and at Kew one was not allowed to climb trees. In any case, she and Lily had other plans. Was everything to be all right, after all?

It seemed so. When Rowan again paid attention, her mother was chatting quite happily. "We used to be just the same. If Mother was going out, we simply vanished till the coast was clear. Once, we must have been very small, four or five — Lizzie and I were caught, Mother took us to the Rectory. We were sent out to play in the garden — I remember old Mrs. Nisbet telling us not to pick the nuts or pop the fuchsia buds —"

"But you did?" prompted Rowan.

"Not exactly. We found a lot of puff-balls, huge things, all dry and ripe, and we had a battle. They burst like bombs, simply clouds of black smoke. We were both in white, our kilts and jumpers — I can see Lizzie now, black as a tinker; her *face* . . . .Poor Mother. She used to say, a woman never knows what shame is, till she takes her small children out to tea."

"Rowan", said Father treacherously, "isn't likely to find many puff-balls in S.W.19?" But Mother, reassured, only answered lightly, "No, nor in Kew, I should hope" — adding after a moment, "What a godsend Lily is!"

Lily's career as godsend went back to the summer of 1942, when Rowan, aged four, was living at Grandfather Izard's farm, Nine Wells, in Ireland. Every day she was turned out to play in safety in the walled garden; and every day, when no one was watching from a window, she would climb the wall and wander off in search of amusement. Soon one of the farm men would

5

be knocking at the back door to warn the elderly maid, Nan, that she was wading in a distant stream, running along the narrow wall of the stallion's paddock, or had crawled into the watch-dog's kennel to stroke the puppies, "the way the bitch would have her savaged, if she found the child there." Often it was too late to save Grandmother from knowing; from an upper window her far-seeing eye would have raked the garden and found it empty, "putting the heart across her," as she afterwards complained.

Then Lily, Nan's fourteen-year-old great-niece, arrived from Kerry to help in the house; and at once it was seen that here was the older, steadier child that was needed — a reliable girl, used to dealing firmly with the young, but not too old to play with them. By no means too old; Lily had been nursemaid to her mother's growing family ever since she could remember, and this new life was a holiday by contrast. Rowan soon found that, far from being a curb on her freedom, Lily was an ally; skilled at bird's-nesting, hopscotch, and making paper boats. The pair would sit in the summerhouse through long afternoons, eating white currants and dewberries, while rain drenched the garden and brought out all the box-and-phlox scents of summer, and the warm smell of clove pinks, like bread-sauce — and Lily's gentle toneless little voice murmured on and on, telling Rowan the facts of life.

Not sexual facts; Rowan would hear more of these in her first week at school than she might have gleaned in a lifetime from innocent Lily. Still, Grandmother might have been startled at some of Lily's home truths. For all

6

her soft speech and quiet ways, Lily liked to make an impression; and she knew a great deal about Rowan's family, much of it astonishing to Rowan. Lily could tell her, for instance, that Grandmother was in fact her step-grandmother, Grandfather having married twice; and that Rowan herself had been left in Ireland, not to be safe from bombs, but to be out of her mother's way, because she was such a disappointment. Her parents had wanted a son to take the place of their first child, a boy who was born dead.

Rowan was astounded. Had she really had a brother once? "Ah," murmured Lily, "you couldn't call him a brother, and you yourself not born or thought of." "But what was his name? And how can someone be born *dead*?" As to being a disappointment, Rowan knew perfectly well, and had always known, that her cousin Ralph, at school in England, was the one who counted in the family. No one had ever hinted at such a thing — not Grandmother, nor Mother, nor Aunt Lizard, on their visits from London; but she knew it was so. It was something to do with the fact that Ralph's mother, in her day, had been the beautiful, important sister; the first-born; the one who counted.

Again, no one ever said this. The knowledge was abroad in the air at Nine Wells, where the three sisters had grown up, playing in the summerhouse, dabbling in the streams, picking double primroses in the wilderness, playing tennis on the grass court beyond the walnut tree, where the grass ran wild now, long and fine, like green hair. Sometimes Rowan fancied she heard their laughter, the creak of a swing, long vanished from the walnut tree, a far-off coo-eee in wet spring twilight, like someone playing hide-and-seek: voices of Rose, who had become Ralph's mother, and then died in China; Emmy, her own mother; and the youngest, Aunt Lizard, still neither married nor dead, and still called by a schoolgirl nickname from her signature, L. Izard. Explaining this nickname, Lily added softly, "Of course, that wouldn't be her real name now. She'd be Mrs. Transen, if she cared to use his name." So, from hints on one side and questions on the other, it appeared that Aunt Lizard *was* married after all. But at this point Lily began to look uneasy. "Well, now, it was a long time ago —"

"But Lily! Where's her husband, then? Oh — is he in the Navy, too?" Her own father, like Ralph's, was away at sea. But Lily shook her head, saying dubiously, "I don't think we'll be seeing that one again."

"You mean he's dead?"

"Well, now, I think he may be . . ." Perhaps, for once, Lily felt she had gone too far. As though anxious to dispose of Aunt Lizard's husband, to bundle him into a coffin and slam the lid, she repeated, "I think so — I think he is," adding — "Not a word to anyone, mind."

No need for such a warning. Rowan had understood from the first that Lily's revelations were for her ears alone. Lily never again alluded to this one, falling back on safer brands of mischief: "Ah, it broke your mother's heart, not getting the boy she wanted. And then you were such a scrap of a creature, she wondered would she ever rear you. And not a kink or curl to your hair, not like any of the family at all, at all." Not like beautiful Rose, Emerald, Lizard, the three laughing ghosts in the garden. Vividly she evoked the infant Rowan, a changeling, wan and fretful, breaking her mother's heart, and soon banished: confidently she prophesied that, if the longed-for son were to arrive now, Rowan's mother, air-raids or no air-raids, would never let him out of her sight.

At four and five, Rowan accepted all this as she accepted her own reflection in the glass. To be told that this was an odd plain child, a disappointment, was simply "what Lily says": the truth, and not yet disquieting. A little later on, gazing dreamily at her companion, it began to dawn on her that even she might have troubles of her own. There was more of guinea-pig than lily in that dumpy figure, sandy hair, meal-white eyelashes. Perhaps *her* parents too had been disappointed? A Lily should be fair, tall and slender, like the row of silver madonnas in the garden. That summer she had noticed these particularly, because of the little metal label stuck at the end of the row to warn off the gardener's fork in winter. She had always supposed that this label said "Madonna Lilies". Now that she could read, she found that it said mysteriously "Lilium Candidum".

And people she began to find equally mysterious. It was not enough to label them "grown up" and expect them all to behave alike. Quite often they seemed to talk another language, of which she could catch only a word here and there; as when Nan and Lily chatted together in Irish. One summer evening, for instance, when friends of Grandfather's were having drinks in

9

the house, a young man cornered Rowan in the kitchen garden and talked wildly to her about his unhappy love affairs, finally bursting into tears, embracing her and begging her to be his little friend: an astounding performance, and embarrassing: her hands were full of lettuce leaves, and she could hear the hungry guinea-pig raging in its hutch, but felt it would be out of place to say so. She was thankful to see Lily coming to her rescue. But, when the visitors were gone, it appeared that for some reason Grandmother was extremely cross with her, although she had done exactly as she was told — listened patiently and politely, for what seemed like a hundred years, and then put up with being kissed by a stranger. She did complain of this in private to Lily, who looked sly and murmured, "That one! He's always drunk as a mouse" — which explained his conduct a little, but did not make Grandmother's attitude less unfair.

By now she was outgrowing Lily's supervision, preferring to be with Grandfather and the horses, or to play by herself in the spinney behind the orchard wall, where no one could follow because the door in the wall would not open. Here, for the rest of her time at Nine Wells, she spent many days of contented dawdling, swinging in trees, nibbling wood sorrel, hawthorn buds and primrose stalks, making grass whistles, catching sycamore keys as they twirled down on windy days in autumn; printing letters to the guinea-pig with a sharp thorn on dock leaves, and endlessly making up adventures or talking to imaginary friends — Rose and her sisters, or people in books. Then some men came to the farm looking for horses to hire for a film, *Henry The Fifth*, that was being made a few miles away. One of them was going to take part in a battle scene. Later he sent them a picture of himself, splendid in chain mail, riding old Decima. Ever after, that mild and amiable mare appeared to Rowan as a spirited charger; and the spinney became a battlefield, littered with hazel arrows.

Lily had lost her authority, but not her power to astonish. In the last winter of the war, in an empty room upstairs, the two girls found a cupboard full of old books and magazines. Jackdaws, building in the chimney, had strewn the hearth with sticks, enough to start their first fire. They carried up fresh supplies, with rugs and a basket of crinkled yellow apples. As the days lengthened and the cold strengthened, they spent their afternoons here, a good blaze drying out the musty piles of *Home Weeklies* and ancient books, relics of Grandmother's far-off childhood. Rowan sped through a clutch of Sunday School prizes, attracted by the delicate little pictures heading each chapter, the ferns and butterflies and dolphins decorating their capital letters; but the stories, with their aura of slums and hymns, she found unspeakably depressing. She tried one called *Ministering Children* — set in the country, with pious children taking comforts to poor cottagers ("On went the happy child, lightly along the snowy lanes") — but the same sense of misery prevailed. When heartless Nancy tossed her spare bread-and-butter to a goat, instead of to the needy, she felt a twinge of guilty sympathy. Giving up the books, she

11

persuaded Lily to read aloud instead from magazine stories. One that enthralled them both was about a sinister child who set out to become heiress to her snowy-haired old godfather, putting various worthy relations out of favour by a series of plausible slanders. But then it came out that the girl's parents were in the plot — they had arranged the whole thing, coaching her from the first in her tricks and lies. Rowan felt this was going too far: no grown-up person would really hatch a plot like that. But, when she protested, Lily, with her knowing smile, told of a woman she knew in Kerry, who married a rich old farmer living up in the mountains. The farmer fell ill with pneumonia, and the doctor said he might live, but he must be kept very warm, with good fires and blankets. But he died. And later, when the rich young widow had gone away, a shepherd remembered that he had passed the farm while the old man was ill, on the very night of "the crisis", and there was a light in one room upstairs, but no smoke coming from the chimney; and the bedroom windows were set wide open, and the snow blowing in . . .

Again, Grandmother would have disapproved. Not that she minded a little gossip herself — all was grist to the mill of her long weekly letters to relations; but she would certainly have thought Rowan too young for such tales. This, no doubt, was why she went out to tea by herself. But, on those winter afternoons, she would be resting downstairs on the sofa, grateful as ever to Lily for keeping Rowan so quietly amused.

Through those later years of the war, the house had come to be run on one precept: Grandmother must be shielded from worry. Growing nervous as she grew older, with planes droning overhead in the dark ("*Wild geese* over again last night" she wrote in letters to London, hoodwinking the censor) — with Emmy, Lizzy and Ralph in perilous England, her favourite grandchild out of reach, the other in her charge, and their fathers, Rollo and Hal, at sea — Grandmother's fears must always be respected. She was afraid of drowning and chills; so in summertime Lily and Rowan would often paddle from morning till night, racing paper boats in the streams that ran down, snow-cold, from the hills; but always out of sight of the house. "What the eye doesn't see . . ." Lily would say placidly. Grandmother was nervous of tinkers, bogs and strange places; so they never told her how far afield they wandered. She was afraid of falls and broken bones; so Rowan, who could not help climbing, had learned to choose remote walls and trees, and her green-smeared jerseys were whisked out of sight by Lily.

Surprisingly, she had few fears about horses, which were the family business. Rowan was taught to ride as a matter of course, and presently to jump. Seeing child and pony on their way to a lesson in the paddock she would only nod approval, and perhaps say later, "Girls soon learn. Poor young Ralph, I remember how nervous *he* was!" In every other way they united to protect Grandmother. Even Grandfather, when she motored with him early in the war, would keep his eyes on the road and away from his neighbours' livestock.

He loved to look about him, and had more than once landed in a ditch. One day, as they set out for Dublin, the car skidded on a sheet of ice in the drive and slewed round facing the way they had come. Grandfather kept his head and drove calmly home again, pretending he had forgotten something. Sometimes, when Rowan got into mischief, someone would threaten to "tell the misthress"; but she knew they never would. Once, people dropped in to tea when, already reduced by mishap to her last clean frock, she had tried to caress a stray goat. The creature discouraged her, but not quickly enough; the frock reeked of goat. Nan and Lily, unsmiling conspirators, scrubbed, wrung and ironed for dear life, in clouds of steam and eau-de-Cologne, to make her presentable. The dear life was Grandmother's: they would not have her worried.

So for both girls, transplanted to London when the war was over, it seemed natural to let Emmy slide into her place as someone who, for her own peace of mind, should not be told everything.

In some ways the change of home made little difference at first. They still saw a good deal of each other. Rowan would have been at school all day, but in her first few terms she worked rapidly through the illnesses she had missed at Nine Wells. Lily, having shared measles and the rest with her brothers and sisters, remained on hand to amuse her. Rowan's father left the Navy and went to work in the City. In his spare time, he and her mother were often out together, seeing friends hardly met, as they said, "since Munich". Aunt

Lizard would now and then whisk Rowan off to the country; once, after summer whooping-cough, to a farm in Hampshire, and on to a cottage on the coast of Dorset — "to be near your Uncle Rollo", Lily murmured. Uncle Rollo, Ralph's father, also home from sea, was now editor of a west country newspaper. But these excursions did not happen often. Left to themselves, Lily and Rowan resumed some of their old ways. Instead of fields and hills, they explored streets and parks. In bad weather, museums took the place of summerhouse or jackdaw room. Emmy, seeing them contented together, and unsure of herself with Rowan, refrained rather wistfully from prying. Like Grandmother, had she done so, she might sometimes have disapproved of their goings-on.

Looking through a shelf of Ralph's books one afternoon, in the restless aftermath of chicken-pox, Rowan languidly picked out *The Green Eyes of Bast*. She was hardly more attracted by this title than by the shabby black cover. No lurid paper wrapper could have given fair warning. She made Lily begin to read it aloud; and from that hour, life was transformed. It was about a demon in disguise, a cat-woman with the habit of taking people for a twilight stroll and then scratching them to pieces. Too late, they would notice the green gleam of her eyes in the dusk. Almost from the first page, Rowan was spellbound with fear, a child possessed. That night she could no more have slept in a room by herself than have (in Lily's phrase) flown to the moon. But hour after hour she kept Lily awake, entreating in whispers, "One more page", and then

15

AWAY TO THE WEST

"Just one more", up to the fearful climax: the lonely victim beleagured in her flat, and the tiny scratching sounds outside as the cat-woman climbed up, *cutting the telephone wire* . . . For both it was the beginning of a new life, a reign of delightful terror. Through the dark days from Hallowe'en to Candlemas Rowan dragged Lily after her in pursuit of the supernatural, the gruesome and the ghastly: fiends, ghosts, werewolves, ghouls of every species. Lily, as childishly obsessed as Rowan, racked her memory for tales of banshees and witches; far more chilling was her true story of a small boy, left behind with another family while his parents were away, who night after night mystified their nurse by screaming that his bedroom was haunted, babbling of headless ghosts, clutching hands, eerie lights on the ceiling. Not till the little fellow had been removed in a state of collapse to hospital did the nurse suspect that all this was innocent fun on the part of her own charges.

The family bookshelves yielded further harvest: a copy of Grimms' fairy tales in stark unsugared versions, with Cruikshank pictures to match. Their favourite produced two slogans — "My treasure, I only dreamt it," and "Go back, young bride: you are in a slaughter-house" — which they exchanged at all hours, until begged by Emmy to stop. At length, in *Ghost Stories of An Antiquary* — the last word as promising as it was unpronounceable — Rowan hit on "Lost Hearts", and demanded it as a bedtime story. Her first reaction, besides pleased approval, was regret that they were not back in Ireland, to visit "the famous vaults of

St. Michan's Church in Dublin, which possess the horrid property of preserving corpses from decay for centuries". But in the night she woke shuddering from a dream of scratches on the bedroom door, "long parallel slits, about six inches in length" — a nightmare blend of Sax Rohmer and Dr. James; and Lily, either conscience-stricken or tired of broken nights, "put her foot down", refusing to read any more horrors. Still the craze ran on for a week or two. Inspecting local churches for vaults, Rowan found a stone carved with a grinning skeleton, and made a detour from school each day to gaze at it with relish. Belatedly, too, they discovered the mummies at the British Museum. Then suddenly the whole thing ended, as quickly as it had begun. Returning from that Saturday visit to the museum, they ran into a youth named Daniel, over from Lily's Kerry village and doing well with a barrow in the King's Road. Lily was still a guinea-pig; but by now, Rowan saw, she had grown into a *pretty* guinea-pig. Next day she blossomed into Daniel's girl friend while Rowan became a lone wolf cub.

Deserted by Lily on the Sunday afternoon, she dawdled back to Ralph's bookshelf, took down *The Wolf Cub's Handbook*, and opened it at a chapter on knots. At once her eye was caught by a story of three people trapped on floating ice and swept over Niagara Falls, because the men who lowered ropes to them from bridges did not know how to tie loop-knots.

This was February 1947. Outside, the great frost held; pavements were banked with grimy snow, ice splintered and curdled beside the Thames. Out walking with her father, Rowan looked down from Battersea Bridge and hoped that history would not repeat itself before she had mastered at least that one vital knot. Ralph came to London at half-term, and found her still frowning over handbook and string. Amused, he took some trouble to teach her the overhand loop. *Knots are quite easy to learn,* wrote the Chief Scout gaily. Rowan knew better. But for Ralph's help, she would never have done it. He also presented her with an old scout knife, complete with cork-screw and hoof-pick. "Now," said Lily, "you're made up for life."

Rowan felt this too. The wolf cub book was not only an antidote to the horror craze: it gave her something she had not known she missed — a succession of practical things to do.

In Ireland for nearly six years she had been learning to ride and climb, to look after animals, hunt for "stolen" hens' nests, light Grandfather's office fire, bake bread and make up butter. She did not say to herself nowadays, as her mother feared, that London life was dull; but, once, started, she read eagerly about tracking, signalling and camping. Skeletons and vaults forgotten, she dragged Lily all over Chelsea and Kensington looking for flags, weather-cocks and statues; and, on Saturdays, to track moorhens and geese in the snow at Kew. In the Easter holidays, free again at Nine Wells, she built a wolf cub lair in the spinney, and stalked hares, larks and curlews in the bogland, hoping to find their nests. Back at school, she started a vogue for acrobatics, which spread rapidly, evoking a new

18

unwritten rule — *No girl may stand on her hands in the lunch hour.*

"It's bad for your inside," explained a mistress vaguely. "Especially you, Rowan. I hear you wouldn't eat your lunch again."

This was true. Since her return from Ireland, a shadow had darkened her life whenever she found time to remember it. Even being a wolf cub could not always make her forget: she could not eat, and in the end she would starve to death. This year, perhaps, before her tenth birthday.

There were several odd things about this affliction. In the first place she had never suspected it until Lily came back from Kerry, having visited her parents while Rowan was at the farm, and told her of a young neighbour who had died in that way. "On her last day on earth she said to her sister, 'Oh for a dinner of bacon and cabbage', and they thought she would get better. So they cooked some and brought it to her, but not a morsel could she swallow. And she turned her head away, and that was the end, poor soul." At school, on the first day of term, Rowan suddenly found she could not swallow the midday cod and potatoes; they seemed to choke her. She smuggled most of her plateful into a handkerchief, and on her way home fed it to a cat sitting on a wall. In the days that followed the cat grew sleeker. School lunch became a daily struggle: first to eat, then to hide the food without being caught. She failed in both. Her mother was not pleased to receive a note from the school, reporting that her daughter was underweight and ate almost nothing; but, with lively

memories of boarding-school meals, she arranged for
Rowan to take sandwiches in future. That was the
second odd thing: food from home, and anything eaten
at home, could be swallowed quite easily — a merciful
arrangement which Rowan did not try to explain.

Another surprising thing: she could forget her doom
for whole days at a time. Perhaps the bracing air of the
handbook helped, as she flicked through the pages for
new ideas, and embarked on a series of unorthodox
"tests". There should, for instance, be a climber's
badge; and the test could be climbing out of the
balcony window, and crawling along the narrow ledge
to her bedroom. It was perfectly safe for anyone who
had spent so many hours on the garden wall, but, to be
safe from interference, she chose an evening when her
parents were out, and Daniel drinking tea with Lily.
Alas, she had reckoned without Mrs. Anson from the
flat below — an elderly, excitable lady, who happened
to return from a bridge party just as Rowan reached the
crucial point in her test: the place where, having let go
of the balcony, she had to walk several feet with sheer
wall on her right-hand side and on her left a sheer drop
of two storeys to the ground. Mrs. Anson's first shriek
startled her so that she nearly fell; more shrieks, and
she was frozen to the spot, unable to go forward or
back. Mrs. Anson stood below, wringing her hands and
calling in turn on God, her husband, Rowan's parents
and the police, none of whom appeared. It seemed that
Colonel Anson, a melancholy man like a Sealyham,
with bushy white moustaches and a roving eye, had
slipped his collar again and gone off rabbiting. It was

Lily who heard her at last, and Daniel who scrambled out to help Rowan to safety, while from the window Lily held out a broomstick for her to clutch.

Neither Lily nor Daniel would have "told". Inevitably, it was Mrs. Anson who did so, in such dramatic terms that promises were exacted, and further outdoor tests became impossible. In London, one saw, there could be no privacy except indoors. She would have to try for the cook's badge, after all, or the house orderly's: not, at first glance, an interesting prospect. Bedmaking and washing-up gained no glamour from artless anecdotes in the handbook about "Goodfellows" and "Boggarts". The idea of a cookery test was better — but not just tea and boiled potatoes. A cake: a sponge cake, with an orange filling, like the one Aunt Lizard had made in Dorset.

Aunt Liz might come to tea on Sunday. Saturday, then, should be the day. And she must do it alone. Cookery, like so many pursuits, became dull with an expert hovering at one's elbow.

On Monday night she took a cookery book to bed and learned a recipe by heart: *The weight of four eggs in flour and sugar* . . . .She could save her butter ration for the filling, but the need for eggs and oranges kept her awake at night. By Wednesday she was driven to confide in Lily, who smiled in her new, complacent way and went to see Daniel, returning with six eggs, four oranges, a lemon and a bag of loaf sugar. Rowan hid them in her wardrobe. Her mother, coming in to say goodnight, took a deep breath — "Heavenly orange smell, I used to dream about it in the war . . ." but once more refrained from asking questions. Only two more days. Only one day. Saturday came at last.

As they made beds together after breakfast, Lily murmured, "Is it right we're to go for a picnic?"

"No, no. My cake . . ."

"Ah then," said Lily peacefully, smoothing a quilt.

And that afternoon, at the front door, Rowan told her, "Mother said she'd be back at seven."

"I'll be in at half six, so." Away went Lily, an overall clasped in her paws, to help Daniel with his Saturday rush.

Now.

She changed into grey shorts and jersey, knotted a green silk neckerchief borrowed from Father's drawer, and lit the oven.

When they first came to London, the gas stove had filled Lily and Rowan with dread. Once Emmy had gone out to the shops, saying, "Oh, Lily, just light the oven, will you, and put in the pie at twelve?" They had a grim quarter of an hour, turning on the gas, throwing lighted matches at the jets from a safe distance, turning off the tap to clear the air, trying again and again. They were almost in tears, when a well-aimed match lit up the jets with a bang. They hid the spent matches in the dustbin and bought a fresh box. But that was long ago. Today, Rowan lit the oven nonchalantly with one match, and began to weigh things on the kitchen scales.

At once she came near disaster. "The weight of four eggs in flour and sugar . . ." but how to keep four eggs from rolling off the scale, while she spooned flour into the pan? There was only a narrow rim to hold them. The book said nothing about weighing the eggs first, then using one of the brass weights; nor did this occur to her. She was holding the eggs gingerly, a finger-tip on each, when the telephone rang in the hall. She jumped. An egg escaped and crashed to the floor. She rescued the other three, and angrily spooned up the broken one into a cup. It was slippery as frog-spawn, but most of it was saved. The ringing stopped. She turned back to the scales. The mishap had scattered her wits, her hands were trembling. But soon she was calm again. The weight of *three* eggs . . . three were easier to manage . . . add a bit for the missing one . . . the rest of the weighing was safely done. She greased two sandwich tins and dusted them with flour and sugar. A good deal escaped to cover the floor and table, but that could be coped with later, preferably by Lily. A glimpse of herself in the kitchen mirror showed her with hair lightly powdered and white eyelashes like Lily's. She spent a few minutes trying to imitate the complacent smile, then recalled herself to her task. Butter and sugar were stiff in the mixing-bowl; she put it outside on the windowsill to catch the sun while she whirred away with the egg-beater, squeezed the lemon, fished out pips and dreamily sucked the skins: then suddenly remembered the bowl. Now the butter was runny like egg-yolk. It had caught a few smuts and a pigeon's feather. She heard Lily breathe, "What the eye doesn't see . . ." and began to fold in the flour; dipped a finger in the creamy mixture, licked it critically, dipped again. It was delicious, like thick cream. No more, she must leave enough to cover the tins. She spooned it out carefully. The gas kept up its rhythmic, companionable whisper. Waves of heat came from the oven, and from the open window.

The kitchen was in deep shadow, but the sun had moved round to shine on a sloping roof outside. Two pigeons woke and fidgeted as the tiles began to burn their feet. They complained for a few minutes, then launched themselves off the roof and soared to a tree in the garden.

The tins were ready. Slide them into the oven . . . snick the door shut gently . . . it was done. Lolling happily against the table, she wiped floury hands on her shorts.

Now the best part: the orange filling. First, you had to rub the sharp-edged sugar lumps over the oranges, so that rind and juice soaked into them, staining the white cubes dark yellow, like iodine on a bandage. A blissful job. She took another orange and tossed it from hand to hand.

The door bell rang.

She started, then stood rigid. Caught out, was her first reaction; her mother was back, the surprise in ruins. Then it dawned on her that Mother would not ring, nor Father, nor Lily. They had latchkeys. The bell sounded again, shrill and urgent: someone was keeping a finger on it. Rowan held her breath. It was all right, she told herself. She had only to keep quiet until whoever it was grew tired and went away.

And then, as if to spite her, the orange slipped from her hand, thumped on the linoleum and rolled across the kitchen. A cannon ball, she thought, would not have made more noise.

The letter-box rattled. A voice called, "Lily, is that you? Do let me in!"

Ralph's voice. She sprang to open the door. Ralph wasn't expected this weekend, she knew. He was supposed to be at a field club camp near his school. Yet here he was, taller even than she remembered, in a greyish sweater that had once been white, and whitish corduroy trousers that had once been grey.

"Hullo, chicken. Where's everyone?"

"I'm by myself."

"Are you! Look, I want Aunt Lizard's new address."

Rowan stared at him.

"Her address," he repeated patiently. "This studio, you know."

"But — I don't know," she admitted, herself surprised. "I just know how you get there." Black mark for a wolf cub.

"There's a clever. Come on, tell me, quick."

The hall clock struck three. She looked at him in exasperation. Soon he would smell the cake in the oven.

"Can't remember? Never mind. Just come and show me, will you?"

"I can't."

He was taken aback at this wail of protest. Then he grinned.

"Up to something, aren't we? What's cooking?"

"It's my cake."

Seeing nothing to laugh at, she added coldly, "I can't come till it's done." Then, because this was Ralph, she admitted, "It's a wolf cub test."

"How long has it had, though? Six minutes? Now come and do another test — guide badge — show me the way to Lizzie's. Not far is it? I'll have you back before you can say Isabella Beeton."

"No, no, there won't be time. It's too hot to run."

"Who said you had to run? My bike's outside."

She looked at him in despair: with no faith in other people's promises. Ralph took the spare latchkey from behind the hall clock. Still dumb, she found herself racing with him through the front door, down the cool dark staircase; away from the precious cake, out into the dazzling afternoon.

CHAPTER
TWO

Aunt Lizard was a painter. She divided her year between London, Nine Wells and various lodgings in the country, formerly shared in the holidays with Ralph, whose guardian she had been while his father was away. In that snowy March she had taken a garret studio near the river, unfurnished except for a yellow cat named Apricot. Removed with his owner to Chiswick, Apricot had returned five times through the snow, on buttered paws, to his old home. There he would be found in the ash tree outside the studio window, crying to be let in. He would not settle at Chiswick. The owner, admitting defeat, had looked about for a tenant whom he could trust with Apricot. At once, a friend brought him and Aunt Lizard together.

"But I'm quite often away," she told him.

"Well, you could leave a lodger to feed him. Someone suitable, of course."

"A fishmonger, perhaps?"

"I leave it to you," he said thankfully, noting the fine bloom of Aunt Lizard's grey tabby cat, Cuckoo.

The arrangement then depended on the two cats. Would they settle down together?

They did so in their own way. When Aunt Lizard moved in, Apricot took one look, then rushed at Cuckoo with a cry of fury. Taken by surprise, the grey cat bolted up the side of a cupboard and peered wide-eyed from above, awaiting the next attack. It did not come. Apricot, with an air of triumph, turned away and sprang into the ash tree. Cuckoo saved his face by staying where he was. The top of the cupboard became his home. He climbed down gracefully at mealtimes, then returned to his perch, where Aunt Lizard made him comfortable with cushions. Apricot sunned himself in his tree; on wet days he lay on the landing window-sill, curved around the telephone. When it rang, he mewed with it on a high note. Aunt Lizard planted the landing window-box with cat-mint to please him. When it flowered, she said, she might paint it: a study in pale blue, pale green, Apricot. Neither cat ever again acknowledged the other's existence.

The yellow cat was watching from the ash tree as Ralph's motor-bicycle slid into the mews and halted on the cobbles. Two floors up, the studio window stood open. Dismounting, Ralph said, "Is that the place? Up there? Good. She's in."

Rowan, her thoughts at home with the cake, asked idly, "Who's in?"

"Liz is! Who else?"

From the pillion, Rowan stared blankly at him. "But she's gone away! Didn't you know?"

"What!" He burst out laughing. "Isn't it dim? — why on earth didn't you tell me, chicken?"

"You didn't ask that! You *said*, where's the studio!"

"Oh . . . so I did. Where is she, then?"

She admitted slowly, "I don't know — I think."

He laughed, groaned and looked up at the window. "Well, someone's there." A face looked out; not Aunt Lizard.

"Looking after Apricot," Rowan explained. Ralph called, "I say. Could I come up for a minute?"

A voice said softly, unexpectedly, "Blast you," and a key glinted in the air, then clicked on the cobbles. Rowan sprang to pick it up, and led the way through the door and up the narrow stair. These had once been stables, the studio a hayloft; in Aunt Lizard's slip of a kitchen, a stableboy had slept. In the studio, Rowan looked about with pleasure. The sunny end was furnished as a sitting-room. She had helped her aunt to choose a table and chairs in second-hand shops, a carpet flecked in black, pale grey and yellow like a brindled cat, french-grey curtains, crimson cushions. The walls were painted white. A new electric fan whirred on the top of a bookcase, beside a jar of lilac. The north side was like a workshop; it had bare boards, easels, a great window with a high bench all along it, holding tubes, tins, pots and brushes. Rowan sniffed the mixed scents of turpentine, paint and lilac, with overtones of boiled fish — Aunt Lizard would have banished those. A table by the south window was piled with books and papers, and the girl had returned to sit there. She was tall, with thick fair hair drawn back into a black velvet snood. Her sleeveless tunic matched the pale lilac. She looked cool and kind. Rowan thought her beautiful. Now *she* ought to be named Lily.

On the wall hung a portrait of Ralph, aged fourteen. The girl glanced from Ralph to the picture and back, murmuring, "The white-headed boy himself." The remark made no sense to Rowan — Ralph's hair was black — and he wasted no time on it, beginning at once, "I thought Lizzie'd be here?"

"If she were, I shouldn't be."

Ralph frowned, glancing quickly round the room, but Rowan knew he hardly saw it. For the first time she realized that he was simmering with some hidden excitement, some news he could hardly bear to keep to himself: hence this need to find Aunt Lizard. Rowan remembered the signs. He had looked just like this, one Sunday last year, when he burst into the flat, on a special "exeat", to tell the family about a marvel seen by the school field club: a golden oriole. From their talk, it seemed that this must be a rare bird; but when next day she felt driven to ask her form mistress, "What *is* a golden oriole?" she was told firmly, "A halo," and referred to a picture in the school hall: Joseph, Mary, the swaddled Infant and a donkey, each crowned with a gold disc. She felt the familiar sense of bafflement, and left it at that.

Ralph burst out, "Oh — isn't Liz a restless creature? I thought I'd only to find her address — !"

"Addresses are given us to conceal our whereabouts." The girl's tone seemed mocking, her smile entirely kind: but her eyes strayed back to her books.

"Lizzie's are, anyway. Will she be back today?"

"No."

"Then, could you tell me where she is?"

30

She said again simply, "No."

He looked taken aback. "You don't mean that!"

"I'm afraid so." She offered him a cigarette from a packet, took one herself and waited for him to light it, then smilingly struck a match and lit both, while he stared at her. He stammered at last, "Oh! Thanks! Sorry! I'm just wondering —" and did not finish. The girl took pity on him. "I know she's helping to do up a house. Down in Surrey, I think. She's been there — oh, three weeks."

"But surely you've some idea where — if you've taken over this place — ?"

"No I haven't. That's Jane. I'm here just for Whitsun, cat-sitting."

"Then you don't know my aunt at all?"

"Oh, I do indeed. She once tried to teach me art."

Rowan cried, "Oh, then you must be one of Lizzie's chits!"

Ralph and the girl looked at her, astonished, and then broke into delighted laughter. Seeing she had blundered somehow, Rowan scuffed at the carpet, furiously muttering, "Well, Father calls them that." Aunt Lizard gave art lessons at a London school, and some of her old pupils had kept in touch with her and with each other. Their names were well known to the family. Ralph said, "You're not Lesley . . . or this Jane . . . are you Caroline?"

"No, I'm Did."

"Short for Dido?"

"Short for Candida," she said shortly, and blushed, as though for her godparents. But Rowan told herself in triumph, "There you are! That's the same as being called Lily!" This seemed to make up for her mistake about the "chits". Did went on, "I'm at King's College. Exams next week, that's why I'm sweating here."

"Oh . . . then I'm interrupting you."

"Yes," she agreed. She blew a smoke ring, gave it a critical look and said, "I've thought of someone who might know where she is."

"Yes — ?"

"The man who lent us *that*" — pointing to the electric fan. "Liz wrote and asked him to, when the heat wave started. And I made him leave his number, in case the thing blows up."

"Oh, come on, let's ring him. I *must* get hold of her today."

Out on the landing, Rowan heard them dialling, talking, dialling again. She strolled to the window and leaned out to stroke Apricot, who lay stretched at ease along a bough. He gazed at her intently, rippled his furry length like a yellow centipede and mewed in welcome: she and Lily sometimes brought him fish. But now her fingers smelled only of orange. He would not come in. She turned back to look over the books on the table. A curious picture caught her eye, like the moon half-way through an eclipse. Underneath she read, *Frog. Fate-map of the Prospective Areas from the Dorsal Aspect.* She was still puzzling over it when the others returned. They seemed to have been successful; Ralph had begun to tell Did about his motorbike, "a reconditioned Ariel." Rowan interrupted: "What's a *fate-map?*"

"What?" Ralph came to look over her shoulder at the diagram. For a moment he was silent. Rowan thought he must be as puzzled as herself; but the next minute he turned to Did, saying in a queer, breathless tone, "I say! You're doing zoo, are you?"

"As you see."

All at once he was talking at top speed, as though he would never stop. "I am too. Next term, at Dublin. As a matter of fact, I've just been over there to fix it — I've switched from history, you see. Starting from scratch, more or less — I haven't looked at any of this stuff since the Upper Fifth! I haven't told a soul here yet — now I'll have to talk them round. There's going to be quite a row, I expect." He looked delighted at the prospect. "That's why I need Lizzie. I thought I'd break it to her first, and then —"

"Wait, wait!" Laughing, Did put her hands to her ears. "Start again, say it slowly . . ."

Evidently his great news was out; but to Rowan it was still a secret, told once again in a foreign language — but for one fact. She cried jealously, "You've been to Ireland? Just now?"

"I flew over yesterday, back this morning."

"But — you can't have. You were at that camp?"

He laughed, turning to Did again. "I arranged it weeks ago. I wrote to the college tutor and said, could I switch to natural science, and he said, come and talk about it. So I went, and we did, and I have. But I couldn't tell my people beforehand. You see —" he stopped, taking a deep breath. Apricot flumped through the window, and Ralph bent to pick him up, tucked the yellow head under his chin and went on:

"I *am* supposed to go on to camp tonight. But I had my bike at the airport — so I thought, might as well run down here first and tell Liz right away. Then she can pass it on to the rest of them. Well, it's my father who might fuss — he expects me to be a journalist, like him —"

Did had been watching him curiously. She said again, "Wait. You're doing a switch. History to what?"

"I told you, zoo and all that."

"And they're letting you? Your college, I mean?"

"Now they are!"

"Quite a switch, though. What made you change your mind?"

"Yes. Well! That's quite a long story . . ." Perching on the window-sill, he blithely prepared to begin at once; but the cat wriggled free, jumped down and crossed to Did, who rose saying, "Oh yes. Your horrible fish pie . . ." and went into the kitchen. Hearing the creak of the oven door, Rowan gasped out — "Oh, Ralph! Oh! The cake!"

His eyes came back from the diagram; then he too remembered. They took the stairs in three leaps, and reached the bicycle. Rowan was on the carrier, Ralph kicking the starter when the two faces appeared at the window above; the girl still calm and amused, the cat aghast. The bicycle moved, there was time only to wave quickly before it swerved round the corner and gathered speed. Rowan clung to Ralph, shutting her eyes against clocks. They must have been gone for hours. The cake would be a cinder.

They roared into the square and stopped.

"Rowan, I *am* sorry."

They looked at one another across the smoking ruins on the wire tray: though ruin was not quite true, Rowan thought, breaking off a crumb to taste. It was sweet and crisp, a bit like shortbread; and the two rounds were not burnt quite black, except here and there at the edges. The rest was more darkish brown, but paler in places, like some kind of toadstool. It did not look unappetizing. Ralph tried, "Cuckoo'll like it, anyhow. He loves burnt cake."

"I know. And it's not *all* burnt . . ."

They said once again whatever could be said. Ralph hovered, obviously wild to be gone, yet feeling he could not dash off now, right away, after this fiasco. If only he *would*, she thought; there was still time to do the orange filling. That would make up for everything. To speed him on his way, she said, "When you see Aunt Lizard —"

"Yes?"

"I want her to come to tea tomorrow. Is it far, where she's gone?"

"Not far at all. Just Surrey. She's got the car." He fished out a cigarette packet and frowned at the address he had scribbled on it. "Watfield Park. Belongs to a Colonel something." He went to study the road atlas on the hall table. Rowan looked at the oranges, and at the clock. She came to stand in the kitchen door, urging silently, Oh do go, please. Go *now*. It seemed to work: he slapped the atlas shut. "Well! So long, chicken. Thanks for helping. Sorry about the —"

"*Don't tell her about the cake!* I want to tell her."

"All right, all right . . . Well, I'd better start. Supposed to be in camp by nine."

He really is going, she thought. Good, good. Plenty of time to finish after all.

Then, with the front door actually open, he turned back. "Rowan! Are you here all by yourself?"

She gave him a frantic look.

"Where *is* everyone? Where's the rose of Tralee?"

"L-Lily? She'll be back . . . I like being by myself."

He looked at her doubtfully.

"I had my cake to do — my test." By now she wanted to wring her hands, grind her teeth, kick something, burst into tears. If he didn't leave her at once, she would never be done in time. She gave him an imploring look. It seemed to make matters worse. He looked sorry for her. "Oh, but it's too bad of Lily! Leaving you hours on your own. I bet Aunt Emmy doesn't know?"

"But that's the whole *point*. It was my test — a *surprise* —"

"For Liz? Look, I say, why don't you come with me? Bring it along?"

She was stunned.

"I'll run you back by bedtime. Look, we'll leave them a note."

"But," she whispered, "it has to have orange filling. I've got two more eggs on purpose, and oranges and l-loaf sugar . . ."

"Oh, bring the lot, Liz can make it." Misreading her innocent gaze, he added kindly, "You haven't had a proper ride on the bike yet."

Damn and blast him, she was thinking. But she could not hold out against Ralph in this high-handed mood. And suddenly she was wild to go. They tipped cress sandwiches and biscuits from the picnic rucksack, devouring them while they wrapped the cake in kitchen paper and stowed it carefully. Eggs, oranges and sugar went in the side pockets. Writing a note for Lily, Ralph asked, "Where shall we leave it?"

"Oh — on the tea caddy."

"Sure she'll find it? We don't want a flap."

"Yes. She'll make a jug of tea for Daniel." She explained about Daniel.

"Ah then," he mimicked, signing his name with such a flourish that Rowan asked, "Will she be able to read that?" He grinned and printed "Ralph Oliver" carefully underneath.

"Ready? Is that your monkey jacket? Put it on."

"No, no, I'm boiling."

"You won't boil if we touch eighty."

"Eighty?" Reluctantly, she slid her arms into the scarlet knitted sleeves.

"Miles per. Look, the rucksack over it. There. All right? Now."

The motor-cycle stood in shade. The spongy leather seat was cool to her bare knees. Her feet rested firmly, her arms were round his waist, fingers lightly pressing his ribs. They swayed together and found their balance. She gasped for breath as they went gently down the hot street; then they turned west into full sunlight. The breeze at that movement caught her, lifting her hair. Faster, faster. Light and air streamed over her. The wings of the wind, she thought, and shut her eyes.

CHAPTER
THREE

They were in deep shade, cool as a tunnel. Rowan opened her eyes. They had left the main road and were running down a lane between pink and black rhododendron thickets, then woods and fields. She smelled pines, bracken, gorse. On and on and on . . . but suddenly the bicycle swerved and stopped. Over his shoulder Ralph whispered, "Look!" A hare was sitting bolt upright in the middle of the road, ears pricked, watching them. A car came the other way. With a flash of white and ginger, the hare cleared a ditch and bounded across open park land. "He was running this way. Nearly into us," said Ralph. And then, "I wonder if this is the place."

Just ahead, Rowan saw a pair of high iron gates, like black lacework, between stone posts. On either side were narrow gates of the same pattern. Ralph pushed one open and they slid through. He closed it, and came to stand for a moment beside the bicycle. In the distance they saw a square grey house with pillars; set off, like a house in a picture, by billowing white clouds, billowing green Spanish chestnuts, a park with deer. Rowan said suddenly, "Oh! Is this where you lived with Aunt Lizard once — in a house in a garden?"

"No, no, that's miles away, in the Forest of Bere." He mounted and cruised silently down a narrow bumpy road under an avenue of lime trees. On either side, short grass was splashed with yellow and orange lady's-slippers. Swallows darted low, skimming the turf like great blue butterflies. The sound of traffic had died to a distant hum. She could hear only the swallows' quick notes, a grasshopper, the click of garden clippers. Again Ralph said quietly over his shoulder, "Look."

"Deer."

"And another hare."

A man in a faded khaki shirt was clipping a grass verge in front of the house, where a strip of lawn had been mown at the edge of the park. Ralph left his bicycle by the last tree, and walked across the gravel. Rowan waited, watching a door between two pillars, where at any moment Aunt Lizard might appear. It opened: but it was another man who came out. He watched Ralph approaching; they met and talked; now Ralph was beckoning to her. She dropped her pack in the shade and ran towards them. Before Ralph spoke, she knew from his face that they had drawn a blank.

Aunt Lizard had been gone three days. Someone had telephoned one morning, begging her to come — "My son may know where, he took the message." She had driven off at once, promising to return, but they hadn't heard from her since: "I hope she's not deserting us, that would be too bad."

For Rowan, disappointment was side-tracked by surprise. Could this be the "Colonel someone" Ralph had spoken of? She had pictured an elderly person like

Colonel Anson; but this colonel looked quite young and almost frighteningly alert. She liked his thin sunburnt face, keen eye and dark gold curly hair. Not a Sealyham: an Irish setter. This was what Mother would call "a sensible man", and Lily "a lovely man": their highest praise.

Watching Ralph's downcast face, he repeated, "Let's see if we can help. Come along."

A high hall ran the length of the house, with a slippery stone floor. There was a smell of new paint. A chandelier glittered in a shaft of sunlight from the glass door. At the far end was another glass door, framed in magnolia branches, with a glimpse of garden beyond. A stairway curved up from the hall, with an iron balustrade, looped and patterned like the park gates. But the stairs were covered in grey canvas, and the wall above looked dingy, with a banister of grime at elbow level. The colonel said with a sort of simple pride, "Doing it up ourselves. The R.A.F. handed it back last month — complete shambles, of course. We've been at it ever since, just three of us, and then Lizzie came. She's been terrific. Hope she'll be back soon. Here."

He led them into a room off the hall. Dazed from the sunlight, Rowan felt as though she were under the sea. She had an impression of shadowed coolness, height and space, palest sea-green paint. Glass sparkled, red-brown tables gleamed. High windows, rounded at the top, looked out over a lawn bordered by flowering hawthorns, so near that she could smell their wry scent. The colonel began to pour drinks. He handed Rowan a tall cold glass, refreshing to hold as an icicle. "DRINK

41

ME", she thought to herself. She could see Ralph getting ready to say something by way of conversation, and wondered which would win: the motor-bike, or the hares in the park? The hares, it proved; and their host smiled.

"You're the naturalist, aren't you? Liz told me. Shandy? You know, I've often thought Watfield must be named after the hares. Poor Wat, you know? They breed like rabbits here, more or less. Poor Brock, too."

"Brock?" Ralph repeated. "Badgers too?"

"Badgers too. You see those hawthorns? There's a sett just there, twelve feet from the window. We put out stuff every night, boiled macaroni and so on, and sit here and watch them. The airmen did them well, too, I must say — one up to them, for a change. Lizzie's got a scheme for putting them on to hound meal — all our points go on the badgers, so she tells me. Still, we thought we'd leave it for a bit, just while the cubs are small."

"Cubs!" said Ralph in a dazed tone; and again the colonel smiled.

"Come and have a word with Kit, he's cooking the stuff now."

The kitchen would have held Aunt Lizard's garret three times over. It faced east across a walled garden, with pear trees, apple fences, rows of young potatoes. Through this wide window, morning sun would shine on the scrubbed wooden table and dresser, cream-coloured "utility" cups and saucers, hairy brown matting. Now it was in twilight, smelling of soap, fresh mint, vinegar; with a whiff of roasting duck from a

42

cooker. A youth, a year or two older than Ralph, stood at the sink, breaking up twigs of macaroni and throwing them into a boiling pot.

"Kit, these young people want Lizzie."

But Kit was too busy to pay attention, or perhaps deep in thought, resenting interruption: like Did, but less amiable. Not amiable at all, in fact. He barely turned to look at them. One swift hostile glance went from Ralph to Rowan and back; a cold glance, from a cold pale eye. If he had been a horse, he would have laid his ears back. Without any pretence of greeting, he finished snapping the pile of thin white sticks with small sharp sounds, then clapped the lid on the pot and stalked out. Grandmother, in her old-fashioned way, would have brought him up to the mark: "when gentlefolk meet, courtesies are exchanged . . .". His father did not seem to notice. He and Ralph went on talking about badgers and badgers' food, beetles, rabbits and wasps. Rowan half-listened, tilting the lemonade glass in her hand. Ice bobbed against her mouth, nectar ran down her throat. Kit was back, mute as ever, with a slip of paper which he handed to his father. The colonel said, "Here we are. The phone message," and passed it to Ralph, who read aloud, "Please come today. Lesley."

Lesley! Rowan jumped at the name, and swallowed an ice cube. She felt it jamming her throat, felt herself choking to death; then it melted and slid down. Kit was back at the sink, loudly running the taps. He washes his hands of us all, she thought. The man in the khaki shirt appeared, a tankard in one hand, a basket of potatoes in the other. He and Kit began to scrape them. The colonel said persuasively to Ralph, "Stay to dinner and see the badgers. Moonlight later on."

She saw Ralph hesitate, and felt his agony of indecision, before he said, slowly, "You see, sir — I have to find my aunt, somehow. And then get back to camp." He explained a little about the school field club.

"Another time, then. Bring that camera."

The colonel likes Ralph, Rowan thought. Why won't he stay? Silly to miss badger cubs, that he's so crazy about. I know he wants to: but he wants to find Aunt Lizard too, and tell her about going to Dublin — and that "zoo" business, whatever it is . . . Yes: he seemed resigned to going. He had pulled himself together, he was thanking the colonel, then saying goodbye to Kit, who gave no sign of having heard, but turned to take the pot from the stove, tipping the macaroni into a colander. Steam rose from the seething mass of white worms. Kit gingerly picked up the colander in both hands. For one second Rowan thought insanely — he's going to sling it at us! But he only shook it, and put it down. Panic and relief must have shown in her face. The grave and silent man with the tankard looked closely at her, and then winked, as though he had read her thoughts. A reassuring wink, and not grave at all. Still, she was glad to get away from Kit.

They were out in the sun again, walking towards the lime avenue, standing beside the motor-bike while Ralph said, "A reconditioned Ariel — we can keep them at school, our last year." The talk became technical. Rowan put up her hand, drew the paper from

Ralph's fingers and read the name on it. Lesley. Lesley Black. So she had heard it right.

Lesley was one of the "chits". Last year, on their way to Dorset, Aunt Lizard and Rowan had stayed with her and her husband Denys, on their little farm under the Hampshire Downs, Packhorse Farm. They had planned to stay only one day — because, said Aunt Lizard, as they drove round the Devil's Punchbowl in her small open car, men can never do for long with their wives' friends. But Lesley would not hear of this. They were her first visitors. And she had a hundred things to ask Aunt Lizard about, from bread-making to book jackets. She made them stay five days. It was marvellous, she said, to have their own home at last, and be in it all day, doing the things you had planned. All through the war, of course, she had been working. First as a woodcutter in the timber corps; and then, after she married, as a tracer at a naval drawing office, stationed in a country house, while she and Denys lived with his mother and stepfather at their main farm, Clare Hall, on the other side of the county. Now they had Packhorse Farm to themselves, and a little cottage, set among larch and hazel copses. Wide pastures sloped down to a railway cutting, the steep sunny banks thick with honeysuckle and wild strawberries. From the orchard, Rowan could watch little trains slide in and out of a tunnel, a dark arch cut in a green hillside.

Lesley had been brought up on a farm, but in the prewar slump her father had moved his family to London, where he now worked for a firm that sold farm machinery. She had looked forward eagerly to the old life she remembered from childhood — for instance, to keeping hens, as her mother had always done — but it seemed that times had changed more than she realized: "Denys says that's all over, the day of the farmer's wife tripping out to the orchard with a bucket of chick food." So instead she planned to earn money in her spare time as a freelance artist, designing book jackets, or perhaps illustrating books. "Though," she told Aunt Lizard ruefully, "a lot of people seem to have the same idea. You can't buy the *Writer's and Artist's Yearbook* anywhere this year. Sold out, they said at the bookshop, long before it was printed. Still — *some* of us are bound to make it, I suppose!"

Afterwards, in London, Rowan overheard a strange conversation. Aunt Lizard said to Mother, "Poor things! One wonders how long it can last." Mother murmured something in reply, and Aunt Lizard said musingly, "Lesley's very romantic, you know, I think she married him because he's so miserable. Girls are geese, they will do that, and then — they find they're the *cause* of all the misery."

"But he seems quite a sleek young man. What has he got to be miserable about?"

"Oh — his farm, I suppose. It belongs to the mother, and the stepfather's taken over."

"Well, can't he start on his own?"

Aunt Lizard said, "Oh, well — capital? It's not so easy . . ." And Mother, after a minute: "He should have found a rich farmer's daughter. Not a penniless artist!"

"*Yes,*" said Aunt Lizard very quietly.

"Still. She doesn't sound unhappy?"

Aunt Lizard said, "Whistling in the dark," and they talked of something else.

Rowan could not remember hearing Lesley whistle, but she had never met anyone less unhappy: in contrast to her husband, silent handsome Denys Black, who was apt to look haggard and gloomy; though, when Rowan mentioned this in private, Aunt Lizard said briskly that English farmers, however prosperous, often looked like that.

Lesley was small, brown-skinned, with short dark curly hair. She wore a thin silver bracelet shaped like a tiny snake, and her clothes were never what Rowan thought of as married women's clothes. For one thing, the colours were often unexpected. Rowan had never seen anyone else wearing pale blue with pale green, or nut-brown with campion pink, or a pink jersey with a bell-shaped purple skirt like a fuchsia flower. Yet she made no effort to appear elegant. Once, running out into the rain, she had snatched something from a drawer to cover her head, an odd scrap of cloth, striped in scarlet, emerald, violet, black. Unhemmed, rough edges hung down in a fringe; but on Lesley it looked like a scarf in *Vogue*. She had a habit of wearing her husband's sweaters, and these too were in unusual colours, sea-green, primrose, russet: "Because I buy them for him," she said proudly. "Before me, they were all flea colour or cold boiled spinach." The sweaters, though so much too big, did not look clumsy but like a charming new fashion. Rowan would remember this when, a few years later, they *were* a new fashion. She also had a furry knitted jerkin, designed by herself from a bumble bee, in wide bands of black and dark gold, with a black hood; but Denys complained that this made people turn round to stare in Winchester, so she gave it to Aunt Lizard.

Her handsome husband, her curly hair, her clothes, her cottage — Rowan found them all enviable. One room upstairs they had decorated for a nursery. Walls and ceiling were tinted silvery-blue, like the inside of a mussel shell, and on one wall Lesley was painting a seascape: rocks in the foreground, a strip of yellow sand, rippling waves that seemed to stretch away to the horizon. So far it had no occupant and only one piece of furniture, a wooden cradle, painted white and decorated with tiny green sea-horses. A camp-bed was put up for Aunt Lizard. "No use starting to alter the other rooms," Lesley said regretfully: "because really Denys can't wait to move. He thinks it's a bit squalid, living in a cottage. Mr. Falconer's going to let us one of the big farms soon." So she was saving her curtain dockets for the new house; but from a country house sale she had brought home a great pile of old muslin draperies. Washed and starched, and bleached on the orchard hedges, they gave an effect of airy freshness and prettiness to the cottage, set off by the dark woodwork, green rose leaves at the windows, a framed sampler, a white Victorian counterpane embroidered with faint pink lilies: "Mother dug it out of some ancient trunk, it's been there since before the Flood." Still, Rowan liked her own bedroom best; a mere cupboard, brown-panelled, just wide enough for a bunk. It was like sleeping in a nutshell. The round window at the end might have been bitten there by a fieldmouse. She was sorry to leave.

Perhaps, as Aunt Lizard had predicted, Denys Black was not sorry to see them go. One could see that, as Lesley said, he was far from happy at Packhorse. No wonder he had to be away a good deal, distracting his thoughts at market, or race-meetings, or playing golf. One day, when he was setting off for the races, Aunt Lizard urged Lesley, "You go too! Rowan and I will be quite happy here." But Lesley said that Denys and his friends liked going on their own: "I don't want to tag along." When Rowan suggested following in Aunt Lizard's car, to give him a surprise, Lesley retorted, "He might be more surprised than delighted": so that Rowan wondered if she had once tried this, and it had gone wrong. That could happen — as she herself had learned through catching a bat in the summer-house and taking it upstairs for a surprise, when Grandmother was ill in bed.

From the way Lesley spoke of him, Denys sounded rather gay and dashing; but only once did Rowan know him to make a joke, and that was puzzling. Sitting hidden at the top of a tree with the cowman's white kitten, Queenie, watching the distant trains, she became aware that Denys was just below on a haystack, doing something to a tarpaulin. She heard the telephone ringing in the house, and a moment later Lesley ran out calling him. But, instead of answering, Denys had crouched down and lain there, still and watchful, while Lesley ran from garden to cowshed, on to the field gate, and then back, calling him. He made no attempt to show himself. At last Lesley gave up and went back into the cottage. Now, Rowan thought, he would spring up and call. However, he did not; presently he sat up and went on quietly with what he had been doing. Nor did he mention it later, so far as she knew. It could only have been meant as a joke: if he wanted simply to dodge a caller, why not tell Lesley? But for some reason Rowan did not like to remember this incident. Something about it, a sense of treachery, made her uncomfortable. The rest of the visit was cheerful, with smells of baking bread, boiling jam, and the tang of green walnuts that she helped to prick ready for pickling, so that her finger-tips were brown for weeks. Back at school for the last few days of term, she was flattered to be accused of smoking.

Once, when Denys was away, the three went for a painting picnic to a hill with a windmill, and drove home at dusk, with a new moon in the west. Rowan suggested, "We could wish," and Lesley said unexpectedly, "I *have* wished. Oh, yes — and a hunter for Denys." Rowan wished to stay there again, but so far this had not happened.

Now, at the gates of Watfield Park, Ralph said, "I wonder if your mamma knows this Lesley?"

"*I* know her. I can take you where she lives. I've been there. Sussex, I think." Better not say she knew the name of the farm.

"Sussex! Have to run you home first, then. Hop on."

"Run me *home*?"

"Yes, and I shan't get to camp at this rate. I'll stay the night with Liz, when I do catch up with her."

"But — you need me, to show you the way. Like the studio!"

He gazed at her, and burst out laughing.

"Don't tell me you can't remember *this* address!"

"No, but — I remember how to get there. A place called the Devil's Punchbowl — and then a long way down the Portsmouth Road — and then we turned off by a hill with a windmill . . ."

"Oh, I expect I can find that."

At her silence he protested, "Look. I can't just kidnap you and take you off, all round the moon, as Gran would say. Aunt Emmy would be furious."

"We can ring her on the way. We could *ask*." She added quickly, "You did promise. The cake — you promised I could take it to Aunt Lizard!"

"Oh, but — fair's fair — I thought she was here!" Ralph hesitated, and was lost. Yes, the cake: he *had* let it burn. He began to accept defeat. "Well — we might ring Emmy, I suppose. If we can find a phone-box. Ready?"

With any luck, she would sleep that night in the nutshell. They set off at a brisk pace for the main road, the telephone, the windmill hill and the Blacks.

CHAPTER
FOUR

At least, thought Rowan, they had found the windmill.

They sat on the hillside, sheltered by a copse. The dark ruined mill stood up against the blue night sky. The sails were gone. Cornfields, ploughed in wartime, covered the hill, leaving a ring of turf like a moat around a castle. A breeze brought alternate waves of chill air and dry heat, soaked up all day by grass and trees. Twilight had changed to moonlight. Ralph and Rowan had made a fire, meaning to cook the eggs for supper. Alas, the eggs were broken, the rucksack pocket awash with yolk. Nothing could be done about that. It must have happened at Watfield, when Rowan pitched down the bag in the shade.

Some time ago she had admitted, "I don't think I can find the farm tonight." Already it was dusk; they seemed to have been roaming for hours around little country roads, all looking alike, none leading to Packhorse Farm. They met no one to direct them. They had paused at a four-way crossroads, reading signpost names by the light of Ralph's headlamp. Something was wrong with the light; it flickered, dimmed, came on again: anyway, the names meant nothing to her. She was looking for remembered landmarks, a lane bordered by copses, a paddock among hazel woods, a green pond, an orchard with a white kitten. Ralph said, "Well . . . perhaps it's a bit late now to go knocking people up." She waited, dreading that he would finish — "We'd better go back to London." But after a pause, he asked, "I say — are you famished?"

They had expected to find Aunt Lizard long before suppertime. Waiting in the red hot telephone box, while Ralph put through the call to Chelsea, Rowan had thought of her favourite supper; bacon and eggs, with thick crisp lettuce sandwiches. She pictured Lesley's kitchen, red curtains and table-cloth, blue Devon pottery, geraniums in the window. She would actually be seeing them again, in an hour or so — if only Mother didn't say, "Bring Rowan back at once!" Ralph was talking rapidly; and then her mother's voice came over the line: "Well! I don't expect to keep either of you long away from Lizzie!" But she did not sound cross; Ralph bent down so that Rowan could listen better, catching the smile in Mother's voice as she added, "Go carefully, won't you, Ralph? No speeding . . . And don't bring back any livestock this time, please. No caterpillars or hedgehogs. Promise?" When she rang off, they looked at one another in triumph. Ralph pretended to mop his brow.

That was hours ago, in the streaming evening sunlight. Night had taken them by surprise. Later, by the useless signpost, Ralph asked again, "Are you famished?"

"A bit." Thirsty, too; but where would they find water? No sign of a stream; no sign of Packhorse pond,

53

either. They were lost, benighted. She had failed. No guide's badge for her.

Ralph said, "Look. We'll go back to the windmill hill and start again at dawn. Perhaps you'll remember then."

He turned, heading north again. Presently the mill reappeared on the horizon, where the sky was still edged with the last sunset brightness. He swung the bicycle off the road, along a narrow track that led through fields towards the mill. They plunged into a dark uphill copse, and came out high up, close to the hilltop, into yellow afterglow. He propped the bicycle by an anthill. They gathered dry grass, thistle stalks and twigs for the fire, and dragged dead branches from the undergrowth. The flames leaped in the breeze, blew this way and that, and settled to a steady glow. Disappointed of eggs, they took an orange apiece, and thought about their mounting hunger. Rowan said at last, "Oh, come on! Let's eat the cake!" She unpacked it, handing over one half. Taking a great bite of her own, she was surprised to find how good it tasted. In the dark one could not see the burnt parts. More warily tasting his own share, Ralph said, "I know — the strawberries!" They had bought a punnet from a roadside stall. They sandwiched the cake with strawberry mush, and he added, "It's a Marie Antoinette sort of supper."

Not just supper, she thought: a midnight feast.

Afterwards they searched again in the dark for sticks, pricking their hands in the undergrowth, and made up the fire. Rowan lay down with the rucksack under her head. One side of her face was hot from the fire, the other cooled by the breeze. Drifting towards sleep, watching the high pale stars, she said, "I know I can find the way in the morning." Ralph spoke quietly, as though to himself: "I keep missing things today. That girl Did — I must talk to her sometime. And those badgers — pity we didn't stay at Watfield, after all."

Half-dreaming, she thought of Watfield, the beautiful quiet house in the deer park, a house in a picture. A jigsaw puzzle picture. All the background was complete, grass and trees and clouds — though there might have been peacocks, as well as deer and hares and badgers. She saw how the colonel fitted in, and the man with the clippers, and Aunt Lizard: "She does love putting things to rights, she likes people to be *taking steps* . . ." Only Kit was a blank. She could not put him together, half the pieces seemed lost. She asked, "Did you think — did you like that man Kit?"

Ralph poked the fire, and she saw him grin in the sudden flare. "Oh! Kit didn't care for us at all, did he?"

"But *why*? When he'd never seen us before?"

"Nothing to do with us, I expect. Had a row with his father, perhaps."

She drifted off again, and dreamed that Kit was a goat. She went to stroke him, as once she had done with a real goat, and he looked at her with glassy eyes, pale and wicked, then lowered his head to attack. She woke with a jump, sat up and asked loudly, "Ralph! Where *are* you?"

"I'm here. You're dreaming. Go to sleep."

"No, I mean — where do they all think you are? Uncle Rollo, and Aunt Lizard, and the people at your school? If you're not at that camp, where *are* you?"

"Yes, well, you have a point there." Teasing voice; but he did not explain. She went on, asking the question that had puzzled her all day — "Why didn't you know where the studio was? Aunt Lizard's been there for ages."

"Yes ..." he agreed. There was another silence. Feeling snubbed, she lay down and shut her eyes. He said suddenly, "I did write to her sometimes, though. Aunt Emmy sent them on. But it's true I've been keeping out of their way — Father and her, all of them. That's why I want to find her now."

"But — she always goes to your sports day?" Rowan had heard Aunt Lizard's comments on this function — always held, she said, on the bitterest day in March — and how she took care to arm herself with a rug, a seat-stick, a flask of boiling coffee and an interesting book.

"I didn't ask her this year." And then, as though the curt words made him feel awkward — "And I bet she was delighted. Anyway, we'll be seeing her tomorrow."

Tomorrow ... The word reminded her of something. A rhyme in some book, about a child who didn't want "today" to finish. It had been running in her head ever since they set out from Chelsea; and "the wings of the wind" came into it somehow, rhyming with "finned", because that was the only useful rhyme for "wind": a fact she had noticed for herself.

The sun was just sinking away to the west . . . that was the first line. Now she remembered the second verse: *She jumped on a flying-fish, silvery-finned: And she followed the day on the wings of the wind: But the dream voices called to her, Little child, rest: Tomorrow the day will come back from the west.*

Tomorrow, and tomorrow, and tomorrow . . .

At dawn a thrush woke her, shrill as a whistle. A cuckoo called faintly, a long way off, and then nearer and nearer, until it came flying into a tree close by. She stood up stiffly, and it flew away with a gobbling sound.

Grey soft daylight lay across the valley. Purple clouds barred the east, streaked with brightness. Starlight and daylight seemed to mingle, hanging like mist in the air. The grass was grey with dew, the breeze keen, as though touched with frost, and with salt from the distant sea. Walking about, she saw cowslips — long-stemmed in the grass by the copse, short on the open turf — but her fingers felt too stiff to pick them. Then it came to her suddenly — I've been out all night. I've slept under the stars. A landmark in life. She could not wait, she must wake Ralph and tell him. Running back to where he lay beside the white ashes, she shook him by the arm, saying, "It's morning! We've been out all night!"

He did not seem pleased: but of course it was nothing to him. He must have slept out hundreds of times. She looked on in silence while he groaned, stretched, sat up and began to rub one shoulder. He muttered "Shocking thirst", yawned and groped in the

rucksack for the last two oranges, threw her one, and
began gloomily to peel his own. Rowan sniffed sharply,
and he groaned again — "Oh Lord. I suppose you've
caught a cold. Emmy'll slay me."

"I haven't. I just — pigs! Can you smell them?"

"Only orange," he yawned.

"Pigs, orange, strawberry punnet —"

"Hen-runs," added Ralph, more amiably, waking up
a little.

"Yes, ugh. And wood ash."

"Motor-bike —"

"You can't smell that!"

"Petrol and oil and tyres."

"Musty old yew trees, I can. Do you remember Jip,
in *Dr. Dolittle*? He could smell things from away out at
sea — bricks in a wall, and kid gloves, and lace curtains
drying — and the hot water someone shaved with."

"And Black Rappee snuff," said Ralph, who still read
this book whenever he stayed at the flat.

"Yes . . . what I meant was, they have pigs at Pack —
I mean, at the Blacks'."

"Ha, yes, the Blacks. Come on, then."

As they freewheeled down the track towards the
road, she repeated confidently, "I know I can find it
now." Ralph started the engine, frightening a yellow
bird in the hedge.

"Oh look — a canary! Was it?"

"More or less." He seemed to have cheered up
wonderfully, now they were on the bike again. They ran
between fields of young corn, and some other crop like
acres of grey lettuce. At a crossroads she said, "Down

here, I'm certain." They went down a narrow road like the farm lane. Staring at open spaces dotted with tree-stubs, it dawned on her that these were the copses she remembered near Packhorse, but they had been cut down. All along the hedge they passed stretches of concrete; Army parking-places, Aunt Lizard had told her. In the spring before the invasion of Europe these little green lanes had been crammed with tanks, great guns, armoured cars. Now the concrete stands were slowly breaking up, weeds thrusting through the cracks. A little car was parked on one of them, a tent pitched near by. Now they came to a paddock, closed in by uncut hazels, and Rowan cried out — "Oh look! Oh, Denys Black's got his hunter. We're there, we're nearly there!"

A tan-coloured colt had raised his head to watch them from the paddock. So Lesley had had her wish! Further on, just round the corner, they would find the farm. She clutched Ralph, begging, "Do stop, do, I want to look . . ." and twisted on the carrier to admire the colt. Ralph stopped. The colt, seeing their interest, tossed his handsome head, broke into a canter, pulled up short with a clumsy half-stumble, and took a few more faltering steps; then paused, dropping his head. Ralph exclaimed, "Did you see? He's lame."

"Yes . . ."

The colt made a cavorting movement, as though ready to dash skittishly away. This time it stumbled badly.

"See that! What's wrong with him?" Ralph asked. "Picked up a stone, d'you think?"

She fumbled with her belt and unhooked the scout knife. "Look, isn't that a hoof-pick? For taking stones out?"

Ralph stared at an object on the knife, curved like a button-hook. He broke into laughter. "I always thought that was a joke. What on earth do we do with it?" But a lame horse wasn't a joke. He took the knife. They moved together towards the paddock fence, and the colt swerved and hobbled away. She stopped, unslung the rucksack and took out the bag of lump sugar. "Do let me — he looks like Squirrel. Let me try."

The colt watched her advance, and eyed the lumps of sugar on her outstretched hand. Very slowly she went on, then stood still, calling, "Come on, Squirrel . . ." — pretending this was an old show pony at Nine Wells, and willing the colt to be soothed by the pretence. He glared, white-eyed. He was not deceived; but he knew a sugar lump when he smelled it. He stretched out his neck, took a step, paused, and came on, sidling and stumbling, ready to shy away if she moved. She did not move. The soft lips were on her hand, nuzzling the sugar, knocking it to the grass. She stood, letting him stoop, grope and crunch, while he tossed his head up and down. Then with her other hand she offered the whole bag. He seized a mouthful, backed and paused again to crunch. She followed one step, and gently took the halter. He showed no panic now, but again thrust at the sugar bag, one eye rolling cynically at her. Ralph was at his other side, taking the off forefoot in his hand, turning it back to look at the unshod hoof, blackish-grey and horny. The colt dipped his head, dribbling sugar over Ralph's ear. Not flinching, Ralph said softly, "There it is. I can see it."

"Stone, is it? Come *up*, Squirrel. Can you —"

"Trying," he grunted. "Wedged in a bit. Hang on to him, won't you? Now then . . ."

Suddenly he set the foot down again, and stood up, very red in the face, patting the tan-coloured neck, holding something between thumb and finger. She cried, "Whatever is it? A *bead*?"

"Marble." She took the little glass ball, staring at it in surprise. She had never seen one before. It was a pretty thing, greenish-blue, with a scarlet thread twisted through the centre.

"Oh, can I keep it? I wonder how it got there?"

"How indeed?" He began to laugh helplessly. " 'Scouting for Boys!' God, I was terrified. Weren't you? I thought he'd kick us both to bits."

"Couldn't, on three legs . . . could he?"

"So they say, I've never believed it. Here, leave me a bit, you gluttonous beast." He snatched up the bag, took one sugar lump and scattered the rest on the grass. The colt turned his back on them, munching away until the last grain was gone; then followed them towards the fence, not stumbling now but walking proudly. Looking back, they saw him watching them with head erect. He blew wistfully through his nose, and Rowan said, "I bet they're pleased with him." But Ralph was looking along the lane towards the farm. "H'm. The point is, will Lizzie be pleased with *us*? How far now?"

"Nearly there."

They walked, Ralph wheeling the bike. Here was the farmyard. She skipped ahead through the gate, joyfully recognizing the cottage, pig-yard, cowhouse, and the little shed where the white kitten used to sleep. She ran to look over the half-door.

The result was startling. The shed was now a henhouse. As though Rowan had been a brown-haired fox, twenty hens set up an alarm, first yelping in chorus, then by turns, strophe and anti-strophe, cackle, shriek and counter-shriek. Rowan stood still in dismay. A man appeared round the corner of the shed, a collie bouncing at his side. Ralph shouted above the din, "Sorry. Are you Mr. Black? I'm looking for my aunt —"

"In my henhouse?" He frowned at them both. The collie took the chance to stand up and peer over the henhouse door. The din at once redoubled. Hens took wing in frenzy, collided in mid-air and fell screaming to the floor. Feathers blew about. The young man yelled at the dog, which came meekly to heel with a fox-like smirk.

The farmer was eyeing Rowan with suspicion: one hand was doubled in her shorts pocket, holding the marble. At his look, she held it out defensively. Did he think they were campers, stealing his eggs? The same thought seemed to strike Ralph. He said coldly, "Your horse had picked that up. The colt in the field, back there. He was dead lame."

"What!"

"All right now. We took it out. I say, aren't you Mr. Black? We've come to see —"

62

But the farmer was gone, racing along the lane towards the paddock. The hens' chorus died to faint bickerings. Ralph said, "Oh, well, we're here. That's something."

"Yes, but," said Rowan, "that's not Denys Black."

CHAPTER
FIVE

The farmer could not thank them enough. They were taken aback at such gratitude. Bad enough, he said, if Suntan had been his own; but he was looking after the colt for a polo player. If the marble had splintered in his hoof, Suntan might have been ruined: a bad start to his farming. "Little brutes from the army huts, cutting across to school that way. I'll give them marbles when I see them!" All this in the cottage kitchen, while he was hacking rashers from a side of bacon and setting them to fry over a primus.

In London an egg for breakfast was a treat, two eggs unthinkable. The farmer scooped up double handfuls from a vast bucket of eggs, broke them into bacon fat, tossed the shells under the sink and fished extra knives, forks, plates and cups from a crate in one corner of the kitchen, absently blowing off straws, dust and cobwebs before he banged them on to the table. Rowan caught Ralph's eye; both were thinking — if Aunt Lizard had been there, the things would have been purified several times over before they came anywhere near a table. But this free-and-easy housekeeping seemed to them delightful, and even Aunt Lizard could not have produced more delicious bacon and eggs. Rowan felt she had never known before what it was to be hungry. No wonder gipsies and tinkers, who slept out every night, needed huge meals of poached chicken and rabbit.

The young farmer basted the eggs lavishly, while with the other hand he tilted the kettle into the teapot. Tea ran red-brown into thick white cups. There was farm butter and dark quince marmalade in its pot, sent by his mother. Only the bread was different from last time, Rowan noticed: not like Aunt Lizard's crusty wheaten loaves. It came in thin pale slices from a wrapper labelled "Farmer's Prize", and seemed to taste of the wrapper.

The Blacks had left in the autumn, it appeared. This farmer had come in March. A big company had bought several local farms, and he was assistant manager, getting experience. His own people farmed in Wiltshire, and he'd had two years at college, and then four years at sea. When he left the Navy, his family had been keen for him to stay at home for a bit, but he found he soon got fed up with that: "You want to get off on your own, run your own life — you know!"

"Yes," said Ralph with feeling.

Her third egg defeated Rowan. She found the collie at her side. It cocked a long muzzle over her plate and licked up the egg. The farmer aimed a cuff at it and went on talking to Ralph.

Looking about her, Rowan saw how changed the kitchen was. No curtains or window plants, no coloured rush mats on the brick floor, which no longer shone with red polish. Breakfast was set on clean sheets of the

Hampshire Telegraph: a good idea, she thought, providing something handy to read at meals, and pictures to look at: she began to read the captions: "First batch of displaced persons arrive from the Baltic States . . . four miles away, at the former Free French camp, Polish troops are preparing their own hostel . . .". Then, under a picture of a beaming child: "Air raid shelter is his home. When his playmates at the council school ask 4-year-old Robin where he lives, he merely points to a surface air raid shelter at the side of the playground. His father has installed electric light and a fire grate and a small coal stove . . ." That sounded attractive, like the snug little homes set up by roadmen in London streets, with glowing braziers, steaming kettles, tea-mugs; but sleeping under the stars had been better still. She skimmed another page — "Lesser-known facts about air raids" — which said that Portsmouth civil defenders had 19,000 spare coffins left over from the war: the sort of titbit which, a few months ago, she would have saved up to share with Lily. Just as she thought this, the word "guinea-pig" caught her ear. Surprised, she began to listen.

"That's just what I was — a guinea-pig."

The farmer repeated blithely — "They might have let me out, but for that. I never stopped being seasick, never, not for a single day. I was about as much good in a ship as my Aunt Fanny, but I came in darn useful all the same. The muck they tested on me . . . ever been seasick? It's true what they tell you, at first you're afraid you'll die, then you're afraid you won't. Most of the chaps would be all right after a day or two, but not me.

I thought they'd leave me in the Indian Ocean, sewn up in a bag, our last trip. And it couldn't happen too soon."

What saved his life, he said, was a sort of trick he found out for himself, lying half-dead in the sick-bay. If only he could keep still, with his eyes shut, he would sometimes drift into a kind of trance, "and get away *here*. Oh, not here really — I'd never seen Packhorse then — but I'd concentrate like mad, thinking of home on a morning like this, grass and cows and buttercups. I swear I could smell it too — you know the way elder and nettles smell when it rains? Then I'd sort of lose hold and find myself back in a bunk, sweating and heaving. But I got better and better at it. In the end I could stay in a trance a whole day at a time. And," he put down his cup and stared at the two listeners, eyes bright and narrow in a healthy freckled face — *could* he ever have looked wan and green? — "I made up my mind I wouldn't die after all. I swore I'd stay alive and come back, and really see England again. The room I sleep in here, a little box of a place upstairs — there's a window in it just like a porthole." Rowan nodded to herself. "Sometimes I wake up now, and I think I'm *there* still — just for a second — and then I remember, and I look out of the window, and . . . you see, *I've made it*!" He blushed to his ears, buried his face in his teacup, and began vigorously scraping out the marmalade pot, avoiding their eyes. Ralph fed bacon rinds to the collie. It struck Rowan suddenly — I don't believe he's ever told anyone any of that before. Looking out of the window, at the sloping fields and the green trees full of birds, she saw it all with new eyes. The farmer looked out, too, "Ruddy bullfinches," and went on casually, "Of course, it takes a lot of men that way, getting demobbed. The minute they're out, 'Back to the land,' they think, and 'Don't fence me in', even if their last job was stoking a furnace in Stoke-on-Furness. Specially then, as often as not."

"Yes," Ralph agreed. "My father, for one. He couldn't wait to dig himself in, down in the west country. Not farming, though. Local papers."

"Oh, well, that's different. The best sort of life, I think, working in the country — so long as you know what you're taking on. D'you know, last time I went home, I travelled down from Salisbury with an old boy who'd spent thirty years in the City, then he got ill, and his doctor told him to get out and do something light and easy. So what do you think he was going after? A market garden, of all things, down in Cornwall. Daffodils and violets . . . a real rest cure, he thought it'd be. Strolling about in the dewy morn, tying up nosegays for market. Poor devil. You can't tell them."

"I suppose not . . ."

"I wished he'd come and stay with my neighbours first. Now there's tough going. Eight acres and a bungalow, strawberries and lettuce, and a sixteen-hour day, some days. I met the chap in the Navy — married a Wren — both as keen as anything. They'll be all right, *if* they stick it, and *if* the gratuities hold out. But last winter — you can just imagine. There they were, snowed up for weeks, running out of fuel, and the baby getting ill, and a lot of their stuff killed off."

Ralph asked suddenly, "Then they were here last autumn? Before the Blacks went?"

"Oh yes. You want to find these Blacks? Come on, we'll go down and ask — pity my tractor man's away, he'd have known for certain. Just a tick, though, let's sling the crocks in the sink, I'll have a go at them later. Plenty more in the crate, but I've never got around to unpacking properly. No time, once the thaw came. Mother's threatening to come up soon, too — I'll have to get on to it before that happy day."

Outside in the brilliant morning, the farmer began with enthusiasm to describe his plans for the next three years. Ralph had to steer him back towards the market-gardening neighbours. Following them along field paths, Rowan heard his brisk and cheerful voice half a field ahead, running on about his crops, about "under-sowing with rye grass" and spraying weeds with "hormones", and "watching out for the sugar-beet — don't want a blasted heath." How different from gloomy, haggard Denys Black; though not, perhaps, so interesting.

The red brick bungalow lay among glasshouses and strawberry fields. The strawberry plants had survived, after all, and the fruit was ripening. Rowan caught glimpses of scarlet and pink among green fruits, white flowers, dark leaves. There was no other kind of garden, only a concrete yard. A mountain of boxes, stained dark red, was piled lightly near the front door, beside a clothes line full of tiny garments. Ralph and the farmer paused as they came near, and seemed to hesitate. Overtaking them, Rowan saw why. Inside the bungalow they could hear a baby screaming. Much worse, its parents were having a quarrel — in different rooms, it seemed, from the pitch of their angry voices. The three visitors heard in high carrying tones, above a clatter of washing-up, "I used to be an officer and a lady, now I spend all my time in the sink" — and began, with one consent, to retreat. Too hastily: Ralph collided with the line of washing, backed away and caught his sleeve on one of the strawberry boxes. He tugged, and they crashed in all directions. The voices were abruptly silent. Even the baby stopped crying: as though someone had smothered it, Rowan thought, though she knew this was unlikely. There was a short pause, then a man appeared in the doorway, a tear-stained infant in his arms and a rather fierce expression on his face. Ralph had been cursing himself under his breath. Now they all looked at one another in silence. Then, as the baby's face puckered ominously, the farmer began at top speed to explain their errand. The young father forestalled the first whimper with an expert hitch and swing, distracting his child's attention long enough for him to mutter, "Somewhere near Winchester, I think. No, wait a sec — was it Alchester? Hang on, I'll just — er — my wife would know . . ." But Ralph cried, "Alchester! No, no, don't bother, please — I know people near Alchester. I'll drive over there and find out." With relief on all sides, they escaped back into the Packhorse fields.

It was not so easy, however, to escape a tour of the farm. The farmer clung to his audience. Ralph seemed cheerful and, for the moment, resigned. Rowan left them to it. The tour would take a good while, she knew, remembering visits to farming friends in Ireland. Now was her chance to look for the white kitten.

She sped to the orchard, revisiting with pleasure the trees she had climbed before. In the hedge she found a thrush's nest with eggs, and a single wild rose among masses of tight green buds. But of Queenie there was no sign. A gaunt white cat, lean and tough-looking, was perched on the white wicket-gate, under a white hawthorn bush. Against the snowy blossom it looked old and dirty like town snow. Its tongue, pink as a wild rose petal, rasped with an ugly sound over the coarse yellowish coat. Rowan put out her hand to stroke it. Feigning surprise, the cat looked up, gave her a brief hostile stare and fled, spitting. But with the stare there had come recognition. This creature was Queenie, grown up.

Depressed, she went back to the cottage, hung about for a few minutes, then stole inside and upstairs, bare boards creaking under her tread, to see the nutshell again. Here it was, at the top of the stairs. The door stood open. This at least was just as she remembered, wide enough to swing a hammock, though not a cat. The ex-sailor might have thought of that. A hammock would match the porthole window, adding to the thrill of waking to find himself safely ashore, a farmer, and no longer seasick.

The blankets on his bed were neatly folded. In his own way, one could see, he liked order and comfort: only the frills had to wait, and the washing-up. She could see the sense of that. But, peeping into the other rooms, she thought again how changed it all was. Lesley had really gone. There was hardly a reminder: no fluttering white curtains, only dust and cobwebs. In the nursery, luggage was stacked up, hiding the seascape wall — packing-cases, kitbags, a tin trunk. No trace of the Blacks. They might never have lived here at all. The wonderful visit might never have happened.

CHAPTER
SIX

The sun blazed over wide fields by the sea. A light wind was blowing, and windbreaks of poplar trees shook their young leaves with a sound like running water.

Ralph turned through a gateway, along a narrow road between plantations of young fruit trees on one hand, rose bushes on the other. The air smelled of late apple blossom, early roses, distant salt marshes. After the ride through shady lanes among the downs, so much space and brightness were dazzling. Rowan shut her eyes, then opened them as two different waves of scent broke over her. First the bike swerved past a barnyard full of young pigs, contentedly grunting together, and then just ahead she saw a beanfield, flowing up to a garden hedge that screened a small round cottage. By the gate, Ralph switched off the engine and went to knock at the door. No answer. He came back and sat beside her, looking quietly about. Something in his face made Rowan cry out, "Oh, I know, I know! It's the spring house!"

She gazed at the cottage as though he had rubbed a lamp and conjured it out of the air. This was where he and Aunt Lizard had sheltered during the war. She had made her aunt describe it many times. Now every detail seemed familiar: the walls of grey flint, the tiled roof, the little chimney, three diamond-paned windows, the well in the garden. She could even see the black bootlace that served as a door latch. Aunt Lizard and Ralph had come here in April 1941, after the fearful nights of bombing that Londoners called "the Wednesday and the Saturday". For the rest of the war, Ralph had lived here in the holidays, sometimes with Lizard, sometimes with friends from school.

Now, as he began to explain, she interrupted — "Yes! *She* told me! About that air raid in London, when you got bombed out of the flat — and you had to go to shelter, scrunching over broken glass, with bombs dropping — and you had a toad in your pocket, and you kept reading to her, all about *adders*!" She laughed, as Mother and Aunt Lizard had done when they talked about it. But Ralph looked taken aback.

"Oh Lord — did I? What a bind I must have been."

"No, you weren't. She said —" Rowan hesitated, recalling, rather late, her grandmother's maxim, *Never repeat what people say.* But surely this was safe enough? "Well — once, at home, a man was talking to Aunt Lizard — he wanted her to go to America, and she couldn't because of your holidays, and he said something about 'a handicap'. And she said, 'He's not a *handicap*. He's my only child.'"

She had felt so sure that this was a joke. She remembered perfectly her aunt's airy smiling tone. But again he did not laugh: much worse, he looked away, across the fields, with a moody scowling expression that made her heart sink. But a moment later she was saved.

There came a snort and a scuffle of paws from the cottage garden, the gate was pushed open and a dusty spaniel ambled up to them, uttering friendly barks. At once Ralph was off the bike, clasping the spaniel round the neck, rolling with him on the ground, crying "Speedy, Speedy, good old chap," whacking him so that clouds of dust arose from his coat, while the dog yowled in an ecstasy of welcome. Ralph told him, "A fine watchdog you are. We might have made off by now with the spoons and the grandfather clock." Then to Rowan, "It's all right, he *is* living here — old Tacker Brooks. He's had Speedy from a pup. He'll know where the Blacks are. Knows everyone, old Tacker. I expect he's off for his Sunday pint, but he won't be long, I can smell his dinner cooking."

The windows were shut fast. Tacker, Ralph pointed out, like most outdoor workers — countrymen and sailors — liked fresh air in its proper place, outdoors. But from inside, perhaps through chimney and keyhole, there seeped a pleasant smell of stew, with bacon in it, and a good many onions. Breakfast seemed a good while ago. Ralph picked two bean pods from the field. They wandered about, munching the little beans, while he showed her places in the garden where he and the other boys had built an ice-house, a brick-oven, a kiln for drying home-grown tobacco: "We thought we'd make our fortune with that." On the south wall of the cottage was a peach tree they had planted. It had tiny green fruits, covered, like the inside of the bean pods, with silvery fur. He drew water from the well, and they drank from the bucket like horses. As they sat on the warm brick coping of the well Ralph asked, "Do you like lizards?" Following his pointing finger, she screamed and jumped clear, colliding with Speedy, who had followed them for a drink. Looking back, she saw in a hole in the coping, just where her leg had been, a slim brown head and glittering eye.

"Oh, ugh, I thought it was an adder."

"Nonsense. Common lizard. They live in the crannies. Come and look." She went, still wary. In Dorset, at Derwen Head, there had been adders on the cliffs. On sunny days, Aunt Lizard had made her wear gumboots.

The lizard slid out of sight. Ralph put his finger into another crevice, brought out something and stared at it, saying slowly, "I say . . . I'd forgotten all about these." Rowan saw what seemed to be scraps of glossy china, yellow, brown, dark red. "Bits of Roman pavement — or I used to think so. There was a Roman villa here, we were always ploughing up bits and pieces — I had a whole collection of them in that hole. Fancy, they're still here."

"Like that hoard you left in the hollow tree!" He had pointed this out on the way, in a shady lane, after stopping to let a thrush finish cracking a snail on the road.

"Yes — and that wasn't the first. I left another at Hurst Castle, in that forest — oh, nine years ago, now. I meant to go back . . ."

"When will you?"

He laughed, shook his head. "Look, over *there*," nodding towards the spinney, "That was where I had the mouse sanctuary. Harvest mice. Come and look."

They crossed the garden, past apple trees and potato patches, into the shade of ash and hazel trees. The ground was covered with moss, primrose leaves, bluebells and wood sorrel. Chewing a sorrel leaf, she said, "It's just like —" she stopped.

"— the wilderness at Nine Wells," Ralph finished.

It was her turn to be taken aback. "But — I never knew anyone else got in there! The door was locked!"

"I climbed over the wall, of course."

"*You* did! Did you?"

Looking at him, she realized that he had not always been six feet tall. She remembered — "There were mice in there, too . . ."

"And red spiders, did you find? And those snails in the wall, with brown and yellow shells?"

Both were pleased at this discovery. It was an unexpected link.

Among briars and hazel twigs he showed her an old tangle of wire netting, all that was left of the mouse-run where he had kept harvest mice, to be safe from cats while he watched them and made drawings. Aunt Lizard, he remembered, had been busy for their first year or two, painting all the flowers in Shakespeare, to be published in a book in America. Sometimes he would help by finding them for her to copy — "Even the very common ones, daisies and violets and primroses — because people in some of the States might not ever have seen them."

Speedy barked from the garden. They ran back, but it was a false alarm: no sign of Tacker Brooks.

"Mad dog," said Ralph, stroking the spaniel's back with his foot. Speedy was still lying in the shade by the well. He thumped his tail, but did not stir.

"I think he missed us."

"Yes," Ralph agreed, "and wouldn't fag after us. Typical."

They sat in full sun on the wooden doorsill, leaning against the door. On each side of the step grew a thick mat of blue speedwell, gay as forget-me-nots in a garden: this was Tacker's flower garden. Larks sang overhead. Beyond the gate the bean plants swayed, their leaves blue-green on one side, grey-green on the other; the flowers somehow bee-like, heavy with scent and with bees. Their black and white colouring pleased Rowan. Once her mother had had a dress like that, striped; she had always liked it. Looking down, away from the dazzling light, she saw that the speedwell was full of ladybirds, and began to coax them on to her hand. Watching them, Ralph said lazily, "When I see a ladybird, I suppose I ought to think, '*Adalia bipunctata*, feeding on *Aphis Fabae*'. What I do think is:

In the cowslip pips I lie,
In the rain still warm and dry,
Day and night, and night and day,
Red, black-spotted clock o' clay."

"One of yours?"

"Did I write it, you mean? I wish I had."

"Aunt Liz said you used to."

"What a lot Lizzie tells you! No more poems for me, though. I'm going to be a serious zoologist."

After a minute he said with sudden excitement, "I'd have missed the boat too, but for Manson. Our biology master. When he started the field club, he asked me to help, and I said I didn't believe in field clubs. Well, I still don't. They're all right for a bit of fun, but you really only see things if you go by yourself. Except sometimes, of course — like the badger sett at Watfield. And he said not to be a fool, that was all very well, but there wouldn't *be* any wild life left for you to watch, if you went on like that. You have to get *masses* of people interested, he said, so they won't let everything get wiped out, or poisoned, or built over. It stands to reason, if you think of it. So I had to help. Well, then, last term, half-term, he took me on a mouse course for students, first-years mostly, at a school near us. And it was shattering."

Speedy rose and came towards them, flopping companionably, with a groan of utter weariness, on Rowan's feet. Ralph scratched the silky head with his toe and went on, half to himself, "I've never felt such an outsider. I don't believe anyone there had ever even *seen* a live mouse, not a wild one anyway, but they knew everything else, all the stuff I didn't know, bones and weights and measures and species. Such an ignorant fool, I felt, and it suddenly hit me — of course, that's what I ought to be doing! Not Causes of the French Revolution, and all that. And I was terrified, I thought I'd left it too late — I nearly had, too. I've been in a spin ever since — but now it's going to be all

79

right." He laughed, adding, this time to Rowan, "So no more poems. I leave all that to you."

"I can't. But we have to keep learning stuff, for English prep. Browning."

"Browning! At your age? No, wait, let me guess — '*Rats!*'"

"Yes, that one, and horses. 'How They Brought The Good News'."

"Oh dear yes. We did it with Merren McKay."

"There's another good one, not Browning —

Riding at dawn, riding alone
Gillespie left the town behind —"

"Go on."

"Trumpeter, sound to the Light Dragons —"

"Dragoons! Cavalry."

She ignored this, preferring the dragons.

"— Sound to saddle and spur, he said.
He that is ready may ride with me
And he that can — may ride ahead."

Reciting that in front of the class, she had been quite carried away, and the girls had rocked with laughter. But Ralph said seriously, "I see. It's the horses you like."

"Going fast I like. The motor-bike too. Where is it?"

"I put it in the shade. Phew, it's hot." They both yawned, suddenly sleepy. White puffs of cloud sailed in the sky. Bees hummed, a cuckoo called, faint and far away like an echo, a cloud cuckoo, a winter dream. Speedy groaned in his sleep. Tacker Brooks, clanking up on his bicycle half an hour later, found all three fast asleep on his doorstep. His shout of surprise and welcome roused them.

"Young Ralph Oliver, well I'm darned! Only talking about you t'other day." Ralph jumped to his feet. The old man looked up at his height with amazement. They were very glad to see each other. Tacker, second horseman on this farm, was an old friend; their first friend here. Rowan saw a spry little man like a jockey — which he had been, she knew, in his youth; and a ship's cook as well. His face was lined like a withered leaf, teeth long and brown, hair wispy. He wore corduroy breeches, quite unlike modern corduroys, laced around the tops of his boots; and a neat hacking jacket which would have fitted a boy of twelve. Over one shoulder he carried a sack.

"Cor, you've grown a bit, ha'n't you? We said last week we'd have to send for you, with all these mice in the beanfield. Never knew such a lad as you was for mice, a year or two back." He pushed open the door, waving them inside.

Rowan stood still in the middle of the floor. She pinched her left hand with her right, and she was still awake. She was *inside* the spring house. It was just as she had pictured: the round walls, whitewashed now, so that she could not make out the rabbit frieze that had been there once, before the war; the fireplace, with two bubbling pots hung on hooks from the chimney; the view from each separate window. Only the furniture was different. Aunt Lizard and Ralph had brought things from Chelsea, rugs and curtains and a rocking chair. Tacker made do with one kitchen chair, one cupboard, a table, a bench. A black shaggy-looking rug covered the hearth. Everything looked neat and shipshape; no washing-up stacked here. She could not see any grandfather clock.

Tacker set his sack down carefully beside his bunk, under the west window. Something brown was crouched in a box near by. She saw a saucer with remains of bread and milk. A kitten? No, a hedgehog. Tacker explained, "He clears up the cockroaches, night times. Regular pest, some years, cockroaches."

"It used to be daddy-long-legses," Ralph said, "and mice, in the winter. Long-tailed field mice."

"Ah! Now then." Tacker began to tell them again about a strange kind of mouse that had been digging up the beans. "Not ordinary field mice, though. Pretty little beggars, all yellow round the throat, like a hunting stock, and a proper shine on their coats, and artful! Seems a shame to go trapping them."

"You've caught one? Oh, where is it?"

"Well, that's the trouble. I'd one or two dead in traps, and then I got one alive, in your old box trap that you left here. That's when I thought of you. I made sure you'd be along one day this summer, like you said on your Christmas card. So I kept it, it was getting quite tame — and I chucked the dead 'uns out —"

82

"And Speedy killed it?"

"Not him. Blighter got away," admitted Tacker. "I'd just opened the door a crack to feed it, and it was gone like a flash, away across the floor, with me arter it. But I never see where it went, in the end. Out the window, I dare say."

"Oh," said Ralph, looking dazed.

"Never seen one like it before, though. I thought you'd like to see it, such a boy as you was for mice. Very rare, would it be?"

"Yellow-necked mouse. De Winton's mouse," Ralph said slowly, "I bet. And I've never seen one either."

"Well, you hang around, and you will. Stopping down The Race, are you?" Tacker took a small square box from a nail. "We'll set this right away, and you come over tomorrow morning —"

Ralph came out of his reverie. "Oh, I can't. We're not staying. We just came to ask you . . ." He told about their search for Aunt Lizard.

Tacker rubbed his chin. "Denys Black. There *was* a Denys Black, farming over Harden way for a year or so."

"That's the one! Hasn't he moved near here?"

"Can't say I'd heard that." Tacker looked at the trap in his hand, then brightened again. "But time we've had dinner, it might come to me. Must have known you were coming — I've a lovely pair of rabbits in the pot. None of your grey squirrels, that they're always on at us to eat. Might as well eat rats and ha' done with it." He took the lids from each pot in turn, clapped them back, kicked the fire to a blaze, filled a third pot with water from a crock and set it down to heat. "There's a gooseberry pudden on the boil too. First of the season. I always have the first goosegogs, Whit Sunday."

Ralph stammered, "Oh, we can't. We'll have something in the village, I've got to go for petrol . . ." But Tacker was not to be thwarted.

"What would Miss Izard think of me, letting you go off without your dinner?" To show himself ready for guests, he took knives and forks from a drawer, and put plates to warm by the hearth. "Tell you what, we'll set the trap right away, you never know your luck." He baited his invitation with a yellow-necked mouse, and his trap with bacon rind. It was a box six inches square, one end fitted with small-meshed wire, the other with a wire trigger that would bring down a hanging door. "Now, I'll just scrub a few more taters, they won't take long on the boil."

"Here, Rowan, you can do that — let's try our luck with the trap, now we *are* here!"

Tacker brought a bowl and knife to the trestle table, and scooped up potatoes from a basket. They were newly dug, satin-skinned, like oak-apples. The skin slipped off at a touch, like peeling a willow twig. Through the window she watched Tacker and Ralph picking their way down a bean drill into the middle of the field.

A faint sound made her turn. From the open door a thrush came hopping over the floor to snatch a beakful of bread and milk from the saucer. The hedgehog stirred in its box and each turned a sharp eye on the other. The thrush flew off. Something stirred and rustled in Tacker's sack in the corner. A ferret? Speedy still lay fast asleep by the hearth, tongue lolling with the heat.

Tacker brought in a sprig of mint and put the potatoes on to boil. He and Ralph went out again at once to look at the motor-bike. She could hear the conversation which began, "A reconditioned Ariel . . ." Sitting on the step, chewing a mint leaf, she pretended to be living here by herself, with the spaniel, thrush and hedgehog for companions, and perhaps a yellow-necked mouse; but not the ferret.

Tacker ladled out generous platefuls of rabbit, onions and buttery potatoes; then sluiced the plates with hot water from the kettle to serve again for pudding. Passing her plate for a second helping, Rowan suddenly realized — I've never once thought about *swallowing*. Not here, or at Packhorse, or at the midnight feast — and only that minute at Watfield, because of that lump of ice. I must be cured.

Perhaps this journey with Ralph had broken the spell. Perhaps after all she would live for years.

All through dinner, Tacker and Ralph had been gossiping about old friends, farmhands, land girls, a forester, a mole-catcher. Now Ralph again began to press him about the Blacks. Had Tacker been an Irishman, he might presently have remembered something out of sheer politeness; but his goodwill took another form. He was pretty sure, he said, that they couldn't have come to these parts, or he'd have known about it. Seeing that Ralph was really set on finding them, he would not urge them to stay longer; but advised Ralph to go across to the stables cottage and question young Bob, the head horseman's son, now a travelling tractor driver — "he goes all over the place, ten to one he'll put you on to something." As a parting gift he opened the rustling sack and took out a large live crab, "for Miss Izard's supper, when you do catch up with her": adding, as he wrapped the crab in dock leaves and stowed it in the rucksack — "Now mind you come back soon as you can, and I'll have one of them mice for you. Don't you forget." Ralph wasn't likely to forget, she could see. The box trap was still empty. That rare mouse made one more thing he was having to miss. They both left the cool and shady spring house with regret, and Speedy saw them off with a dismal howl.

And again, at the stables cottage, they drew blank.

Waiting on the carrier, in a strip of shade by a greenhouse, Rowan picked a dandelion and made a whistle, winced at the bitter taste, then picked two plantains and made them fight until one head flew off. She looked up to find Ralph beside her. He said briefly, "All out or asleep," and then, "So they got the greenhouse mended at last!"

"Mended?"

"Don't tell me that's something Lizzie never told you! Not about our buzz bomb?"

"Oh, the spring house wasn't bombed? She never told me!"

"No, it wasn't, nor the stables either. Funny thing, blast. But all this glass was smashed to bits."

It must have been in 1944, he said, on the first day of the summer holidays. Aunt Lizard had come across to the greenhouse for tomatoes. He was in the spring house, and he heard a buzzing, snarling noise, and the place started shaking like a station with an express going by. He rushed out and saw the flying bomb ("doodle-bugs, we called them then") whizzing along, and it came right over the spring house. Then the noise stopped and it went into a dive. Ralph had thought it was falling right on to the stables. A great crash and roar, and it disappeared — into a soft patch in the marsh, but he didn't know that at the time. Then there was an awful silence, except for the thudding of horses' hooves in the paddock. "I'd never run so fast in my life. And when I got here the greenhouse was in ruins, jagged bits hanging and the rest a great pile of splinters. And I thought Liz was under that."

"Where was she?"

"Oh, in one of the stable cottages, chattering away. They'd never heard a thing till the bomb fell. Old George was livid, frightening his horses like that." The memory made him smile, but after a moment he added rather wearily, "I wish we could find her now. I just don't know where to ask next." Frowning, he looked away towards the downs. Rowan looked too, and exclaimed, "Oh, is that where what's-her-name lives? You know — Merren? That has a keeper's cottage?"

It was a lucky shot. His face lit up.

"Merren! Of course! Why didn't I think of that? Do you know — it's just struck me — ten to one that's where she is, all the time. Not with those Blacks at all."

He added a shade grimly, "She'd better be, too. It's just a matter of time, now."

"Till we find her?"

"Till Manson sets the Garda on me. Eighteen hours adrift!" He laughed, and kicked the starter.

CHAPTER
SEVEN

She was not there.

They rode up a deep lane between wild rose hedges, past a chalk pit, to the top of a high crest crowned with slim birdless trees. On the other side a grass track ran downhill, then up again by a valley dark with yews. Ralph had to push the bike up a chalk gulley, steep as a cliff. He forged impatiently ahead; but half-way up he waited for Rowan, saying again as she came near, "I'm certain Lizzie's there." He let her sit down to rest on the bank beside the path.

Yew trees and rowans, black and silver, wreathed in wild clematis, covered the valley to the west. To the north and east lay open downs dotted with juniper bushes. The green smooth turf was patterned by small scented flowers, mauve and white and yellow. A dry sweetness like herbs spiced the air. Rowan pressed her hands over warm patches of thyme and looked towards the sea.

A mile or so away she could see a village with a cricket match in progress. She gazed at it, fascinated. She thought of country walks with Father when she had watched the start of matches like that; seeing the wicket inspected and approved, the coin reverently tossed, fielders take their places, the first batsmen come out and solemnly pat the crease; hearing the momentous word, "Play"; then the deep hush as the bowler walked away and turned to deliver the first ball. Up to that moment it always seemed as though something exciting were really going to happen. For other watchers, obviously, the mood held; but never for her. In the first few overs she would find the excitement seeping away into flatness. There was no tense struggle after all; only a quiet cautious game that went on for ever, played by quiet cautious men. Soon, in a frenzy of boredom, she would have to wander away, looking for a tree to climb, a ditch to jump, a thistle to knock over; something, anything to do. But now, looking down at the far-off scene, the little white figures, she was glad they were there.

A faint rustling from the rucksack on her back made her jump. Quickly she slung it away. The crab had crawled out of its dock leaves; claws waved from the flap.

"Ralph, look. Poor thing. Shall we let it have a run?" She lifted out the crab and set it down in the shade of a thorn tree. It seemed to watch them from baleful little eyes. Ralph said, "It does look a bit off colour."

"Can't we put it back in the sea?"

"Rather late for that, isn't it? About twenty million years."

"Twenty *what*?"

"Since there was any sea up here." He was still cheerful, certain that they had only to reach the cottage on the downs and their search would be over. He picked up a lump of chalk, licked it, set the crab on his knee and began to scrawl on the red-brown shell. Watching, she read, "A Present —" and interrupted, "Is it far?"

" 'And round about the prow she wrote — ' Is where far?"

"Where we're going?"

"— 'A Present from Beaumarsh.' No, not far at all." He finished this inscription and returned the crab to the shade.

"Is she really there, do you think?"

"Yes, I do think. She often goes there, doesn't she? They were thick as thieves, you know, Lizzie and Merren, when we had the spring house. For one thing, they were both in the civil defending lark. But *I* knew Merren first. She was our form mistress, when I first went to school. Then she said she wanted a rest from boys so she took up being an air raid warden."

"Up *here*?"

"No, down there, in Portsmouth, and she had this cottage for resting in. She'd have it crammed with evacuees, or sailors on leave, or bomb-shocked wardens, and she used to come there on her days off. The evacuees never stayed, of course. Too quiet, they said. Look at that crab!"

It was sidling rapidly downhill. Ralph wrapped it in fresh mullein leaves, and they went on. At the top of the down they turned east, following a wide grass path between fields of young heather, bright green over last year's brown. The sky was cloudless now, the air glittering like a bee's wing. They went through a patch of scrub oaks and young pines, glad of their deep shade. Beyond, a broom hedge took them by surprise. In full flower, it blazed like a line of torches. The light airy scent of broom met them before they were out of the copse.

Merren's cottage, when they reached it, was not quiet. As they walked nearer, a bee spun past with a fierce twang; then another, and another. As they reached the mossy gate, the air was filled with humming, now high, now deep. Sunlight glinted on small wings; black specks danced before their eyes. They hesitated, and Ralph said bravely, "Just the day for a swarm. No wind, no clouds, and it must be eighty."

"Eighty?" It struck Rowan — But I asked him that before! When? Yesterday, in the flat, twenty-four hours ago. It seemed years.

"Eighty in the shade. Do look at that broom!" But the hedge was too bright to be looked at long.

Bees zoomed past, and Rowan ducked. "Won't they sting us?"

" 'They don't sting when they're swarming' — I hope that's true, I'm quoting Tacker. What on earth's that row?"

Above the sound of the bees they could hear a different din, a sharp persistent dinging noise from behind the cottage. They walked under a clump of fir trees, through a wicket gate, along a flagged path, past a well like the one at the spring house, into a tangled garden, with budding roses, poppies, foxgloves. The cottage roof was green with moss. A hen-run held six blonde well-groomed hens, crooning to one another from dust-baths. By the broom hedge, near a row of white wooden beehives, Rowan saw a woman veiled like a currant bush in white net, and a cross-looking wrinkled little man who was walking up and down, beating a kettle with a spoon. As they drew near, the veiled one turned and called in a muffled voice, shouting to defeat the netting and the spoon, "Yes, if it's water, help yourselves from the well. Put the lid back, won't you?"

Ralph stood still and called, "Hi, hi, Miss McKay."

She stared, then hurried towards them, tearing at the veil, calling, "Which of you is it? Russell? Pearson? No, of course, it's *you*, Ralph. Help me off with this damn thing." The veil had caught in a hair slide. She tugged, and a laughing face appeared, framed in short ruffled brown hair.

"It is Ralph, isn't it? You all keep getting so tall. Tall and tame. To think", she said to Rowan, "this great sheepish creature was once a demon in grey flannel, the bane of my life. Your daughter?" she asked Ralph.

"My cousin Rowan — Merren, *where's Lizzie?*"

So they knew by her look of surprise that his guess had been wrong. She had no idea where Lizard was. "Last time I heard, she'd just moved into a studio."

The little man, still beating the kettle, came up to mutter something at Merren. It sounded to Rowan like gibberish; he repeated it, and she realized that he must be speaking a foreign language. Merren nodded and said, "Yes — yes", then to Ralph and Rowan — "You see you're just in time for our swarm! — what luck they've picked today, when Stanley's here to help me. Only poor Stefan, he's had to skulk indoors, bees make a dead set at him, he says. What is it, Stanley?"

The little man brandished his spoon. He looked crosser than ever. Searching for words, he waved his arm towards the hives and the dancing bees. "Me — work." Then, with a furious gesture towards the cottage, "You — *in*!"

There could be no refusal. The three trooped meekly in at the back door, closing it against sun and swarm. To Rowan the place seemed pitch dark, except for a line of light under the door. They could hear Merren laughing softly before she explained, "Of course he's right, the bees love him, he can do anything with them. But he hates anyone watching, let alone meddling. He gets quite ferocious and then I stop . . . Ah well. Tea, I think." She struck a match and lit an oil stove. Getting used to the bluish twilight, Rowan saw that this was a narrow stone-paved kitchen, with a window at the far end looking out into another shady pine wood. The flagstones were hollowed a bit, near the sink and range. Ralph stood by the door, hands in his pockets, head bent. When Merren spoke to him he looked at her blankly, his face very pale in the dim light. Merren peered at him, then turned to Rowan, thrust a table-cloth into her hands and opened an inner door, saying briskly, "Now in there, darling, you'll see a table."

Rowan found herself in a sitting-room, with a gate-legged table, deep shabby armchairs, jars of ferns, a brick fireplace heaped with cones. It smelled like a pine wood. Framed photographs of school groups hung on one wall. Rowan spread the tea-cloth and turned to search the groups for Ralph. Behind her a voice said, "Good afternoon."

She spun round. Another man was sitting on a windowsill, screened by a curtain and a newspaper. He laid down the paper, came over to shake hands and returned to his perch. They looked at each other in silence. Out by the hives, Rowan had somehow taken it for granted that "poor Stefan" must be a nervous cat or dog; and if this were he, there was something catlike about him, apart from his quietness and his tawny eyes. Wary he seemed, yet quite at home; aloof, but not shy. He did not speak again, and Rowan could think of nothing to say; but it did not matter. They went on peacefully watching one another until Merren appeared in the doorway: "Stefan, if you can't face honey, I shall boil you an egg."

"Face?"

"Eat."

He answered carefully, "It is not that I do not like. But with bees I am not *persona grata*. Your hens — the Buffs? Buff . . . ?"

"Orpingtons."

"— they are amiable, they do not sting. Thank you, I will have an egg." His thin face broke into a charming smile.

Merren lingered, and said quickly in a low voice to Rowan, "What's wrong with that boy?"

Puzzled, she stammered, "Wrong with him?"

"Ralph, I mean. Not a word to say for himself. What's this about trying to find Lizard?"

"Oh — we are. At least, he thought she might be here."

"H'm. Seems upset. Sulks, or a touch of the sun, do you think?" Then, as Ralph appeared behind her with a large black cat around his neck — "Mind how you handle Badger. He's a walking rabbit pie. Three young ones last night, if you please — I found the tails on the doorstep. 'Doomsday in fur', with the rabbits. He's been sleeping it off all day."

If Badger were replete, or if Ralph had a touch of the sun, it did not affect their appetite for tea. Ralph sat on the sofa, the huge cat across his knees, sharing scones and honey. Merren was right, though, about his silence. He seemed in a queer mood, deaf and blind, as he had been at first with Did in the garret yesterday. He took no part in the conversation. Merren glanced at him now and again, her look hovering between concern and reproof, but she left him alone. When Stefan spoke of "the camp" it was to Rowan that she explained. He and Stanley were "displaced persons", like the men she had seen in the picture on the Packhorse breakfast table; exiles from their own country, unable to go home, for reasons which Merren did not go into. They were living in a wartime camp near a village at the foot of the downs, still called "the French camp" after its first occupants. Merren, now the village schoolmistress, was helping them with their English, so that they could take jobs later on.

96

Gazing at Stefan, Rowan thought he was the neatest egg-eater she had ever seen. When he sliced off the top with his pocket knife, it was like cutting an orange. Her scout knife could not have done it. She noticed that all the finger-tips of his right hand were hideously scarred and blackened from some mishap, as though he had caught them in a chaff cutter, like young Paddy at Nine Wells. And like Paddy's, the nails had never grown again properly. She thought Stefan had not noticed her noticing this; but he finished the egg quickly and put the hand out of sight. Feeling guilty, she looked away at Badger, who was flaunting a tongue like pink blotting paper, swirling honey from his whiskers; then her gaze went back to Stefan. Somehow one could not help watching him, just as one was drawn to watch the cat.

Merren filled a fifth teacup and put scones in the saucer, wondering aloud, "Dare we disturb Stanley with tea? Ralph — no, Rowan, could you go?" Setting the cup in Rowan's hands, she added, "Not afraid of the bees, are you?" Rowan might have said, "I don't know", or more frankly, "Yes, I am", but she saw that this was an order, not a question. Merren was not a schoolmistress for nothing. Stefan went with her to open the back door, shutting it swiftly behind her.

Once outside, she saw that there was nothing to be afraid of. The bees would not bother to sting her; they had something better to do. The tanging noise had stopped, the humming dancing throng had vanished. Looking about, she saw Stanley on the far side of the garden. As she came near, she realized what he was watching. From the branch of a wild cherry tree hung a living skein of bees. She set the cup on the grass and gazed in fascination at the mass of small brown bodies, endlessly pouring over and over each other in a dark mass like a lump of shimmering resin on the bough. Stanley did not glance at her, but she sensed that he did not mind her staying. Chat and laughter he had resented — this was a serious business — but one silent child was all right. Presently he stooped, picked up the teacup and drank, gazing all the time at the bees like a shepherd watching his flock.

Back in the sitting-room, looking again at Stefan, she found herself suddenly comparing him with the farmer at Packhorse and the colonel at Watfield. Like them, Stefan was wearing old clothes, threadbare and shabby, with leather-patched elbows; the way most people dressed at home. But she thought — rationing or no — the colonel and the farmer would have worn old things anyway, because they were comfortable. She had a feeling that Stefan had put on his best to come here, and made himself as smart as possible. And in spite of his darns and leather patches, she began to feel grubby and untidy beside him, suddenly aware that she and Ralph had done very little washing or brushing today, that her pullover was stained with strawberry juice, her sandals white with chalk dust and her shorts still crumpled from sleeping out on the hillside. She wondered too what Stefan's lost home had been like, and what sort of job he would find now. Clearly, so long as anyone kept bees, Stanley would be all right anywhere; just as Tacker or Paddy would be all right in a foreign country, so long as there were horses.

Something about Stefan, despite his spruceness, his beautiful manners, his careful English, made her remember another story of Aunt Lizard's, about an Arab pony set to work on a farm, embittered, and dying of a broken heart. She wondered if he would ever be "placed" again as long as he lived.

The name Lizzie brought her back with a jump from this reverie. Merren was talking about the old days, and a night when she and Aunt Lizard had been stranded miles from anywhere in the Hampshire countryside: "at Steventon — you remember, Ralph? There was a country house," she told Stefan, "a training place for rescue workers — they'd *built* a bombed street in the grounds, bricks and rubble and beams and broken glass, and cellars with whole houses collapsed in them. It must have been '43 — we were waiting for big raids again, because of the invasion. *Our* invasion. The second front, we called it then. They used to send the rescue squads out there on courses, for practice, and Lizzie and I went for a day. Well, of course that was where Jane Austen lived as a child, so Lizzie and I dashed off afterwards to see the church, and in the end we missed the transport. We had to walk to Winchester, miles —"

"Winchester!" cried Rowan, sitting up.

They all looked at her. She said to Ralph — "This morning, that man, at the strawberry place — he said the Blacks had gone near Winchester!"

"Alchester, he said."

"I'm certain that was *after*." She rushed on — "Because I remembered, when he said it — when we

99

were driving back from Dorset, Aunt Lizard and me — we went into Winchester Cathedral, because of —" she turned to Merren — "something about *her*, Jane something, on the wall."

"Jane Austen? Yes, there's a plaque in the cathedral."

"Well, I thought about that, I remember, and he hadn't *said* Alchester then!"

Ralph was already on his feet.

"It sounds rather vague ..." began Merren. "Shouldn't you be getting back to school? Well, there's a phone-box in Alderton — try directory enquiry — look, if you must go, take a honeycomb for Lizard. Heather honey. Yes, I insist. I'll just wrap one for you —"

Another cry from Rowan, "Oh, the crab! I meant to give it a drink! It must be suffocating, all those blanket leaves." She raced out to the gate where the rucksack lay beside the cycle.

The crab had not suffocated. It seemed to be dozing.

"Dreaming of seaweed at low tide," Ralph said, catching her up. "No, don't wake it — all right, I said goodbye for you — for God's sake, *let's get on*." Suddenly white with temper, blazing with impatience, he squashed the honeycomb viciously into the other rucksack pocket.

The cycle began to slide downhill, away from the cottage and the little pine wood, into brilliant early evening sun. Looking back, Rowan thought Merren was calling to them from the gate, some warning it seemed, but Ralph would not hear. A few minutes later he regretted this. The grass track ended abruptly at a high wire-netting fence, surrounding a new plantation. They freewheeled along the wire, swishing through heather and bracken, picked up a narrow rabbit track, tried that and lost it again. Ralph was cursing quietly to himself. He would not turn. They went on down the slope, weaving among heather thickets, grazing past anthills, bumping over grass tufts and into rabbit holes, running blindly through patches of juniper. She clung to him blindly, head down against the low sun, the switching briars and undergrowth. Excitement turned to doubt, then to alarm, as though they were on a bolting horse; but before panic could set in the ride was over. They were on smooth ground again. Opening her eyes, she found that they had come out on to another wide turf pathway half-way down the hill, running into a farm road that took them through green cornfields to the main road. Waiting there for cars to pass, Ralph looked over his shoulder and grinned.

"Still with us? Whew! Thank God you got us away like that."

She thought in gratified surprise — did I?

"I'd have gone clean crazy if you hadn't — look, Rowan, we've *got* to find her if it takes all night. I'm not going back till we do. That all right?"

"But we are — aren't we? Going to find her, I mean?"

"Yes, but — oh, never mind!" Impatient again: almost savage. But not, surely, with her? *She* had thought of Winchester.

But all grown-ups, she realized, were angry about something as often as not, and Ralph counted as grown up. As a rule one had no idea what it was about, and simply hoped one might not be to blame. The exception was Grandfather, who rarely lost his temper, his one concern being always, "Don't frighten the horses".

Ralph had jumped off now and was running his fingers over the tyres, feeling for bits of flint as though they had been a horse's hooves. That made the motor-cycle more interesting, as if it were alive and in need of looking after. Brushing off his fingers, he laughed suddenly — "Oh, don't they drive you wild sometimes? Good old Merren, I know she means well, but honestly — on and on, all about 'Stanley and Stefan', like some ghastly double act on the radio — as bad as in the flat in the holidays. You know, I just have to get away sometimes. Last Christmas night, they thought I'd gone to bed, I ran all the way to the river just to *breathe*. I was tearing along the embankment and I heard footsteps, someone running after me, and guess what it was? A policeman, wanting to know what was up, was I all right! — he thought I meant to jump in, I suppose. Of course," he allowed, "they're all twice our age."

She had an astounding sense of really taking in, for once, what an older person said. For this was what she and Lily did on winter evenings when the others were out or busy. They would slip out into misty or frosty lamplight and race round the square, or down to Fulham Road, jumping up at trees; or the other way, as far as a gate with a stone fox over it, on the edge of Old Brompton Road. If they were missed at home, Lily

102

meant to say that she was posting a letter, but so far they had been lucky. Now she saw Ralph dashing through midnight streets under the dripping winter boughs and cloudy skies of London night — white clouds sunset-tinted from the vast lamplight below — driven by the same urge for movement that she used to feel at those cricket matches. To have this in common with a tall young man, twice *her* age, was the most flattering thing that had ever happened.

After a pause he said in a different tone, brisk and confident, "Well now. Over to Winchester, track her down, Chelsea next, hand you back to your sorrowing parents, camp by midnight and a bit of badger-watching. What'll you bet?"

"But how? When we still don't know any address?"

"That'll be all right. Let's get over near Winchester, and we'll find a phone-box and start with the operator. They'll know Denys Black, you'll see. They know everyone." He added, as though to convince himself as much as her — "Rollo says you can always find people when you know whereabouts to look, just by asking around. Post offices and pubs and so on."

Post offices will be shut, she thought. It can't suddenly get as easy as that. This time yesterday we thought it would be easy, and here we still are.

But there, as she thought it, they were not. They moved, bumped out of the lane, swerved and gathered speed. For a moment she almost lost her balance, for this time Ralph had turned east instead of west. They ran on with their backs to the sun for a mile or so, then took a north turn. The highway stretched ahead, straight and smooth between flowering verges, a dark blue ribbon edged with green and white.

CHAPTER
EIGHT

Clare Hall lay in the crook of a winding lane: a large house, white-painted, with a broad front lawn sloping down to a stream, and high trees almost touching the roof at the back. This was where Denys Black's parents lived: his mother and stepfather. The Falconers.

Ralph knocked and rang at the front door, waited, rang again, grimaced across at Rowan waiting on the motorbike at the white iron gate; and disappeared round the house, where he found an empty garage. Coming back, he reported —

"Gone for a drive in the cool of the evening. Come on, let's have a look round. Sure to be someone about."

The front door had a fox mask knocker and an electric bell; the side door a black iron ring and old-fashioned brass bell-knob: a "yank-and-clang", Ralph called it. A small black bell with a rope hung outside the back door, over a large scraper and fixed boot-brush. None brought any answer. Their notes died away into silence deep inside the house. From the back door a flagged path led through box hedges to yards and outbuildings. All seemed deserted. Not even a dog barked. They came to the front again and stood there under the blank stare of nine windows. Three of these

105

were attic windows, high up under the eaves. One was a little way open. Looking down to the stream, Ralph said with momentary interest, "A good garden to keep water voles in." He yawned and began to prowl to and fro, once more on the edge of impatience. This check was infuriating. They had found the Falconers' place so easily, just as he had predicted, through a chatty telephone operator. But what good was that, with no one here to direct them? For even *she* didn't know where the Blacks were now. He began another restless circuit.

The house faced west. At the back, under the trees, the cool of the evening had already begun. Petals dropped from a great horse chestnut, crinkled, creamy, each with a spot of pink. A white owl dipped over their heads, hovered, veered away, then floated lightly as a thistle seed, up, up towards the roof. It seemed to pause for a moment under the house eaves like a swallow at a nest, then it was gone.

Ralph breathed, "See that? — it went inside. In through that window." Here at the back too one attic window stood a little way open. They watched; they did not see the owl fly out, yet a few minutes later it reappeared over-head, gold in the light, white in the shadows; and again it hovered by the open window, and flew in. Before they had time to exchange a look, a second white shape was floating softly in and out of chestnut and acacia branches, hovering a moment at the window, vanishing inside.

Ralph whispered, "Barn owls. They've a nest in there — and young ones. And they fly out the front window,

do you see? The attic must run right across the house."
He broke off to listen. A hoarse cry had sounded from
the other side: surprising from one of those moth-like
creatures: like a backyard screech from a Persian kitten.

Ralph said longingly, "I wonder if I could get up
there? I'd love to see that nest."

An acacia tree grew close to the back of the house,
almost brushing the eaves. Next time one of the owls
flew in, Ralph was perched on a branch above the attic
window-sill. Rowan was not really surprised at length
to see him swing on to the sill, push the window further
open, slide through and disappear.

She thought he would be out again at once, but
minutes passed with no sign of him. Perhaps, like the
owls, he would come out through the front window?
She ran round the house and stood on the gravel
looking up. He did not appear. A car hummed along
the lane, nearer and nearer, and she thought in panic —
the Falconers! No, it sped past the gate. But, next time?
They might be back any minute. Reluctant to be found
here without Ralph, she ran back to wait under the
trees. Once or twice she called him. No answer. Should
she climb up after him? She swung herself into the tree.
But half-way up she thought — he might have come
down already, while she was at the front; might have
gone the other way, looking for her? She dropped down
again and ran twice round the house, then doubled
back to run widdershins. Then she remembered a story
from last winter, about a man who chased a spectre at
dusk, round and round a hedge, until it dawned on him
that the thing was chasing *him*. She stopped running.

107

Her hands felt cold and damp, her face hot with sunburn. She walked slowly down to the farmyard, to a little bridge where the stream flowed in from the fields, broad and shallow, before losing itself in the shadowy water-garden. She bent down and dipped her face into the chattering water, down until she could feel the small cold pebbles, then stood up, shaking her head so that cool drops ran down her neck. From the wide white farmyard came a low throbbing hum like a giant refrigerator; but no other sound. The animals must be out in the fields, hens gone to roost, if there were hens. She thought rather forlornly of green stableyards in Ireland, with roaming hens, horses' heads looking over doors, friendly cats in mangers. She pulled a handful of dock leaves for the crab, ran to the motor-bike in the lane, pulled out the drooping mullein and arranged the fresh leaves in their place. The crab still seemed asleep. She closed the straps carefully, spinning out the task for a long minute. Now Ralph *must* be down from the attic. She made herself walk very slowly across the gravel and round the house, keeping away from the trees, out in the open, where nothing could take her by surprise.

He was not there.

Dawdling back the way she had come, past the side door, she stood on tiptoe to finger the brass bell-knob. Her reflection swam up, swollen, like a face on the back of a spoon — frog or goldfish? — with dark, wet rat-tails of hair. She breathed on it, and it hovered in mist, a Cheshire cat. Trying out a grin, she thought someone spoke from inside the house, and put her ear against the door to listen. It had sounded like someone saying, "Hi." Could it have been Ralph — could he have come down that way? She grabbed the iron ring, twisted it and gave a push. The door swung ajar. She was looking into a dim hall, with a passage beyond and stairs going up. No sign of Ralph. About to shut the door quickly, she caught sight of a carriage lamp hanging on the wall, gleaming with brass and glass, like the ones they had used on Grandfather's gig in the last years of the war when the car was laid up. She remembered those lamps flickering in the windy dark on winter evenings. Sometimes one would flare up, spitting out long flames, so that the horse would catch the smell of burning wick and try to bolt. This thing looked more like an ornament, it seemed odd to see it in a house. She stepped over the door-sill to look more closely, and a hoarse voice said, "Goodbye."

She gasped once from shock, and then again from admiration: a parrot was sitting in a cage on a small table: a great green bird with red and white markings on its face. It craned down from its perch to look at her, gave what sounded like a slighting sniff, turned its head from side to side and lowered a white eyelid. Again it croaked, "Goodbye." She ran across to the cage: "No, no, not goodbye, *hello*." The bird closed both eyes with a look of boundless pessimism and repeated, "Goodbye."

There was something dismal in the sound. It refused to speak again, but blinked and eyed her crossly, twitching up and down like an elderly person trying to settle for a nap. She hadn't cared for its greeting; in a

109

strange house it made one feel more than unwelcome — there was almost an echo of that bird in Grimm: *Go back, young bride: you are in a slaughter-house.* She backed away, turned, slipped through the door and ran straight into the jaws of a grey wolf coming to kill her.

That was a moment of nightmare, but only a moment. It hadn't really touched her. A man appeared behind it. He shouted an order and grabbed it by the collar. It checked, glanced round at him and turned slowly from wolf into dog: still watchful and curious, but no longer snarling and bristling. The man spoke to it again, and then to Rowan:

"He won't hurt you. You took him by surprise, see? Best not to move too quiet, really. All right, Flash, all right."

He had the end of a hose-pipe coiled round his shoulder, and the rest of the hose lay along the path, trailing from a garden tap. Water gushed, he began to sprinkle young plants in a stone urn. Everything seemed normal again; she was in a farmhouse garden in calm late evening sunshine, and here was somebody like Paddy, come in to water the flowers and give his dog a run. She felt gay with relief, and confident. In another minute she would ask about Lesley and Denys Black, and he would tell her where to find them. Better still — Ralph must appear soon, and he could do the talking.

The man was looking at her thoughtfully, as though realizing that the Falconers weren't back, beginning to wonder why she was there. Here it came.

"How did you get here?"

110

"Oh, on a motor-bike."

That seemed to amuse him. "On the young side, aren't you?"

"I'm nine."

"Young for a licence — I meant?"

"Oh!" Light dawned. About to explain, she saw the trap: for where, still, was Ralph? He would say, "You came with your cousin: where *is* he, then?" She couldn't answer, "Up there in the attic" — they would be lost, Ralph betrayed, the man would think he was a burglar. She looked so frightened that his tone changed from mild enquiry to suspicion.

"You came on a motor-bike?"

"Yes," she breathed.

"Who brought you?"

No answer. He spoke more sharply.

"Who was it you wanted, then?"

That was easy, and safe. She looked at him gratefully: "We want to know about Denys and Lesley. The Blacks, I mean. Which farm they're on now . . ."

His expression relaxed again. "Ohhhh! Them! But you've come to the wrong shop, my dear." He moved on to the next urn, saying over his shoulder, "They haven't been here, oh, not for a long while."

"But —" She was lost again. "I thought — I'm sure, someone told us, on the telephone —" close to tears, she asked, "You mean, the Falconers . . . *they*'ve gone?"

"The Falconers! Why, no, they'll be back presently."

"Oh, then that's all right. They'll know, won't they? — where Lesley is?"

A queer look crossed his pleasant sunburnt face. He shook his head slightly, then abruptly flung the hosepipe away on to the lawn, where it lay gurgling into the grass. He came up to face her.

"Now let's get this straight. You want to find Denys and Mrs. Denys. Is that it?"

"Yes, we — yes."

"Then you're lucky you asked *me*. I can tell you. But if you'd asked Mr. Falconer, or Mrs. — well, that might be another thing."

But don't they know, then? She didn't say this aloud, but he answered her look. "Maybe they know all right, but they wouldn't say. There's been a bit of a family quarrel, see. A parting of the ways, you might say."

What did *that* mean? And why, why didn't Ralph come? Something must be wrong. He must have got shut in somewhere in that attic, in an old oak chest or a cupboard with a secret lock: or — savaged by a parent owl?

"No need to look scared, there wasn't any bloodshed. Not all on your own, though, are you?"

She shook her head.

"What's the mystery? And where's this bike you came on?"

Thank heaven, that was easy again. She led him across the gravel, the grey dog padding behind them. She swung the gate open and he saw the Ariel. At once, like all the other men they had encountered, he was walking round looking at it, forgetting to question her further.

112

With luck, he would still be doing that when Ralph at last appeared . . .

Ralph at last appeared.

The dog had begun to pant and whine, lying where it had been told but pricking its beautiful ears and pointing up the lane. Down the lane Ralph wandered, with the most natural air in the world; just back from a stroll. He came up to them, saying nonchalantly, hands in pockets, "Ah. Hello. Evening."

"Evening." The man's tone was civil but guarded. The dog whimpered. Ralph said, "That's a handsome beast."

"(All right, Flash.) Good watch-dog. Wolfhound," said Flash's owner. His eye travelled over Ralph, missing nothing: the green dust and the grey dust on his sweater — tree dust and attic dust? — a jagged tear in his corduroys, the questions and reproaches on Rowan's face. His look said — Now, what have you really been up to? No good, I bet. Prowling about.

Ralph said, "Oh yes? Nice breed" — giving him stare for stare, but avoiding Rowan's eye.

The man's gaze dropped to Ralph's pockets. Ralph took his hands out of them, pulling out the linings as though by accident. The man coughed, hid a half-grin behind his hand and said more cordially, "I hear you were wanting Denys?"

"Oh yes. Thanks. Thanks very much . . ."

"They're living down near Bursley. At a training stable, Harry Gregg's. You follow this lane along to the four-went ways . . ." He gave a string of directions. At the end he hesitated and then said, "Denys left off

113

farming last year. He's Harry Gregg's secretary down there. That's a neat job," he added quickly.

The neat job, it appeared, was not Denys Black's but the Ariel. By the time Rowan grasped this, he was crouching beside Ralph on the grass, giving some advice about the faulty lights. But their talk ended sooner than she had thought possible. Ralph was keener than ever to get on, to find Bursley and Aunt Lizard before they had to worry about lights again. Time enough for that.

As they started she just had time to hiss at the back of his neck, "Oh! Where *were* you!" He threw back a brief look of surprise: "Not long — was I?" The surprise sounded genuine. She had felt like a long-lost child in a story, rescued at last. Clearly he had no idea of that. Still, he hadn't got locked in anywhere. Or at least he'd escaped, she *had* been rescued. Perhaps that was all that mattered.

They had passed the "four-went ways". The road climbed steeply and dipped again into a country of rolling grassy plains. Somewhere down there was a house with all the things from Packhorse, put together again. Soon she would see them. She began to sing.

CHAPTER
NINE

The sky in the west was like a high bright window; the moon was up but not yet shining. Ralph stopped at a crowded public house to buy ginger beer and pies: they were thirsty but neither wanted to eat, after all.

On the far side of a green upland they came at length to a tan-coloured five-barred gate, opening to a drive that ran between wooden fences to distant stables.

In the garden of a lodge an old woman sat on a kitchen chair, knitting a sock in a cloud of midges: they must be getting knitted into it. When she came to the end of a row she used her empty needle to swipe at the midges, then as a back-scratcher. She watched intently to see that Ralph latched the gate behind him. Like Lily, Rowan noticed, she could knit away "without looking": as hard in her own experience as riding a bicycle "no hands". Dropped stitches, cut knees, were still Rowan's lot.

Ralph leaned across the hedge. "Do you know Mr. Black, please?"

"Oh yes."

"Does he live here, I wonder?"

"No, he don't."

"Oh — but — isn't this Mr. Gregg's place?"

"That's right."

"But Denys Black — I thought he lived here?"

"No, he don't."

"(Oh God.) Could you tell me, where has he moved to?"

"Ha'n't moved that I know of."

"But you said he doesn't live here now?"

"So he don't. Never did, though." She gazed at him through blank pebble glasses, needles clicking. He watched her helplessly. She came to the end of another row, seemed to unpick a strangled midge, then to take pity on him. She pointed along the drive. "Up there, they live. Top lodge."

"But you said — oh thanks. Thank you very much," he finished meekly. To Rowan he muttered with a grin, "Game, set and match."

She watched him remount, then called, "You won't find him, though."

"Not? Oh, they're *not* away!"

"Him, I said, didn't I?"

"Then, Mrs. Black — do you know . . . ?"

"The artist?" With something between a sniff and a smirk she said, "You'll find *her* all right."

The second lodge was screened by evergreens. Closing another gate, Ralph said, "Hang on. I'll go and look." But Rowan didn't mean to lose sight of him again. She followed along a narrow path overgrown by dank-smelling laurels. A small house crouched behind them. Before they reached the door someone came darting out calling, "Denys!" — and then broke off, and began again haltingly, as though to strangers, "Oh. Sorry. I thought —" but Rowan cried, "Lesley, it's me!"

Lesley stared. Rowan insisted, laughing, "You *do* know me!"

"Of course she does," said Ralph.

"Oh Ralph — Rowan ... How stupid of me. I thought I heard a car ... oh, I'm so glad to see you. I was just thinking, I could not bear one more minute alone."

Alone?

"Alone! We thought Lizzie —"

"Oh, but she's gone to Dorset. Rollo was coming. You know — Derwen — that old coastguard cottage."

"Thank God," said Ralph. "Coastguards *must* be on the phone."

"Not *old* coastguards." When she laughed, Rowan thought, she really looked like Lesley. For in some way she had changed, one could not quite see how. She was smaller than Rowan remembered, and paler; even her voice seemed *less*. At Ralph's groan, she stopped laughing — "Oh, what's the matter? There's nothing wrong?"

Ralph answered strangely. "I don't know. Did you say Rollo's there?"

"Not now, he won't be. He had to go back today."

"Then ... she's down there by herself?"

"There *is* something the matter! Ralph, what is it?"

"It's just — nothing, but — look, Lesley, I think we'd better get on. I do rather want to see her."

"Oh — don't go yet! Please. Stay to supper. Coffee, then." She seemed ready to weep with disappointment. He hesitated, then gave in — "Well, if we may. Just for a minute."

"Yes, yes, come in. Oh, and I've news for Lizzie."

So had Ralph, thought Rowan — but he doesn't care about that any more. Something else, now, he wants to see her for. What else? Just this morning, it was to tell her about that "zoo", and flying to Dublin, and the "mouse course": when did he change? At Merren's, when she thought he was so cross? No, before that. What happened before that? Oh, I'm so sleepy . . .

Curled on a sofa, she suddenly felt sleep closing down on her. She stretched out on the cushions, eyelids drooping, so heavy that she had to let them shut for a moment. Between waves of drowsiness she heard them next door in the kitchen. Lesley was making coffee, telling Ralph something — something about a letter she'd had a few days ago. From Aunt Lizard, from Watfield, asking her to telephone with an urgent message, "Come at once!"

They were laughing together. Sleep vanished, she pricked her ears. Ralph said, "So it was a plot, was it?"

"Well, she needed to get away for a bit and she thought that would be tactful."

"Let me guess. Something to do with Kit?"

"Yes! Oh dear, yes. Kit thought she had designs on his father. Oh, the sulking there was — she said, if she'd stayed another day, she'd have seduced the gallant colonel from sheer exasperation."

Quiet laughter. Then Ralph again: "I thought it might be that. Even Rowan and me ... looking daggers."

"Silly boy. That won't put the women off. More likely to be an amusing incentive — to anyone but Lizzie."

They came into the sitting-room. Eyes still shut, Rowan heard coffee poured, a biscuit tin opened. Ralph was talking about their journey, then about the field club where he was supposed to be, then about some film the biology master was going to make. Water voles, on a river in Sussex — Lesley would remember the place. (Of course, they'd known each other years ago ...) Rowan was floating in the air now, looking in at the attic window. Dark in there. A long way off she heard Ralph's voice, then Lesley:

"Incredible luck. Remember the baby seal at Derwen, the summer before last? Oh no, you were at school, it must have been June. Denys and I stayed there with Liz, we made piles of sketches. Ever seen a little seal? We couldn't take our eyes off it."

A pause, then softly, "Asleep?"

Rowan tried to say, "No, I'm not," but the effort was too much. The voices went on, hushed now: keeping her awake where the louder, casual ones had not. Lesley said some drawings of hers had been accepted for a book, a story about a seal. *The Proud Gunner*. She'd been working at them all the winter — Lizzie's idea, to start with.

"I remember the name. Came out last year? Won some sort of prize? No, I haven't read it."

"I don't advise it really. Too heart-breaking."

Rowan was still floating, but in the sea now, at Derwen. She couldn't open her eyes. The sun on the water was dazzling, like a white lamp on a table . . .

Lesley whispered, "Just finished them when I heard from Liz. So she came down from Watfield and had a look, and she liked them, and we packed them straight off to the author. And she went on to Derwen, and Denys had to go to Newmarket. So I'd no one to tell, when the wire came. Will I meet him next week, about an illustrated edition. With my drawings! Can't believe it yet."

"Lizzie'll be thrilled. One of her gels."

"Oh, and Denys will. We thought I'd have to go back to tracing."

". . . all that way tonight?" Rowan heard next. "Must you? Well, leave her here. Pity to wake her. Fetch her tomorrow?"

Rowan felt utter relief. Now she could sleep and sleep. Putting it off one moment longer, she heard Ralph murmur, "Clare Hall," and "Owls' nest". Then Lesley: ". . . so afraid they wouldn't remember to open the windows!"

"Yes, they're open all right. I've seen the nest. Yes, up in the rafters. Four little squeakers. Of course I could only stay a moment."

At this colossal lie — for he must have been away half an hour! — Rowan was wide awake, sitting up to protest. They laughed at her indignation. Starting to pour coffee for her, Lesley paused to listen, her eyes on the uncurtained window. Darkness had fallen. Far

120

down the drive, car headlights shone, swept nearer, stopped at the gate, flashed through the shrubbery; then vanished. The hum of the car died away. Seeing Rowan's eyes on her, she said quickly, "Oh, I must be dreaming. I thought — but of course — I know he can't get back before tomorrow night."

In the black window Rowan saw the three of them reflected, drinking coffee among the laurels: an eerie picnic. She looked round the room. The furniture was the same, yet it wasn't a bit like the farm. She couldn't picture this room in daylight. Perhaps the sun never came in. She realized: I don't much like this place, I don't want to stay here all night. I'll make Ralph take me when he goes. It's so dark in here. Just now, when I dreamed about that attic — it was here I was dreaming.

Funny: the white lamp was so bright that she couldn't look at it. But the darkness was there, and something else, something lonely and discomforting and, yes, frightening. She prepared for a struggle.

Then, looking at Lesley, she saw there would be no struggle. Lesley wouldn't try to keep her if she didn't want to be left. The trouble was — it seemed mean to go and leave *her*. She didn't want to be alone, she'd said so.

But — Rowan thought — she's living here. Whether she's frightened or not, she has to stay.

CHAPTER
TEN

The road through the Forest was a high branchy cavern, swept by floodlights of approaching cars. Now and then came a lull, when they ran through lichen-smelling darkness behind the small steady beam of the headlight. Faster, faster. She found herself singing lines at random to the tune of "Bonny Dundee" —

"Not a word to each other; we kept the great pace
Neck by neck, stride by stride, never changing our place.
Past Looz and past Tomgres, no cloud in the sky —
So we were left galloping, Joris and I."

He braked suddenly with a shout of warning. A pony was lying in the road ahead. Ralph cruised until the front tyre almost touched its flank, and it rose reluctantly and moved to the roadside. One foot on the road, he said, "Don't buzz in my ear. What are you singing?"

"How They Brought The Good News."

As they moved on, the headlight flickered. When it brightened again he took up the tune:

"I sprang to the stirrup, and Jorrocks, and he.
I galloped, Dirk galloped, we galloped all three.
Behind shut the postern, the lights sank to rest —"

The light went out, and stayed out. He drew in to the verge and stopped.

"What's happened?"

Her foolish question went unanswered. She scrambled off and let the rucksack slide to the ground. He stood up saying pleasantly, "We sang too soon, didn't we?"

There was a long pause.

"Oh well! Daylight in a few hours. Safer then, that's one thing — these damn ponies . . ." Another had appeared, waiting confidently to be fed, then dropping its nose to rummage in the pack. It followed as they groped their way into the forest, then vanished with a reproachful snicker.

They had found a path that led to a sheltered spot, a circle of beeches, a fallen tree, heaps of brushwood. The leafy ground seemed dry, and there was enough light — away from the blinding cars — to collect branches and old bracken for camp beds. Ralph propped the cycle against the fallen tree, and found a burrow where the crab might refresh itself; it was torpid, but he barred it in with a chunk of bark. They lay on pillows of bracken; last year's beech husks pricked their legs. Better not light a fire, he said: someone might take umbrage. Lesley had insisted on lending Rowan a thick woolly sweater as long as a tunic; and the air was warm and still, as though the day's sun made a tent of warmth hung from tree to tree. They did not talk. The beeches stood around companionably, whispering now and then. Alone, Rowan knew, she would have seen a bear in every bush; now the forest felt friendly, far more so than that dark little lodge from which she had escaped with such relief. Moonlight hung like mist between the branches, and made a streak of dull silver on one trunk. Someone called in the distance; or was it an owl? The crowded day overcame them and they slept.

She opened her eyes to a grey dusk; chinks of white light from the sky showed among the beech leaves; whether moonlight or daylight she could not tell. She sat up, cramped, crumpled, stiff with cold now. Ralph had rolled off the bracken and lay full length on the ground, his head on his arms. She was about to stand up when something caught her eye, a few yards away in the bracken. A white blur. She gazed, and made out a dark creature standing there; a bear cub. It was watching her.

Oddly, she was not afraid. Something in its stillness reassured her. She touched Ralph, and he woke with a start. He sat up, dazed, trying to remember where he was. Dead leaves clung to his hair. She breathed, "Look!" and at the same moment he too saw the pale stripe on its head. She heard him draw a quick breath. Still she felt no fear, only curiosity. What could be going to happen!

All the time, while she watched, the bear cub had been motionless, head held low; but now she saw the white stripe dip and rise. She had not taken her eyes from it, yet after that gentle movement it was no longer there.

She whispered, "*Did* you see — did you *see?*"

"Yes."

"It *bowed* to us."

"Yes. And I didn't miss it, that time."

"Miss it?"

"I kept missing them, didn't I? At camp, and at Watfield — it was a badger, didn't you know?"

"No. Oh." Not a bear? They sat looking at the place where it had been.

They had spoken in whispers. Now she said aloud, sharply, "Ralph. It was that flying bomb, wasn't it?"

He turned to look at her in surprise, rubbing his eyes. She rushed on, "At the nursery. That greenhouse that got bombed — that was what made you start wondering. Wasn't it? Wondering if *she's* all right? Aunt Liz?"

He nodded, and began to get up. Peering at his white face, she persisted, "Do you think she is?"

Kneeling, he stared at her as though she had given him a fright. He didn't speak. She whispered, "Are we going to see?" Then — "What's wrong, d'you think?"

He seemed to shake off his heaviness; jumped to his feet, groped in the rucksack and pulled out two bottles, saying rather distantly, "Here you are. Ginger beer, your favourite breakfast. And a pony pie — catch." They ate and drank. Rowan forgot that moment of illumination, forgot to think of any more questions, knowing he wouldn't answer them. She leaned against a tree, watching again for the badger — it hadn't seemed timid: might it not come back? Already the sky was much lighter than when she woke. A branch hung down beside her with young leaves fluttering, pale as honey, damp and crinkled. Still thinking of bears, she said suddenly, "Let's leave it something, the badger, for a present." She dragged the sticky package from the rucksack, begging, "Look, let's leave it the honeycomb. Because it came and —"

"Honoured us. Yes, all right." They laid Merren's honeycomb in the bracken where the badger had stood.

Half-way to the road, they remembered the crab and raced back; but it was gone, the burrow empty. The chunk of bark had been pushed aside. They searched in vain. Ralph said, "The badger must have crunched him up. Poor old chap — I meant to put him back on the rocks, I thought he'd earned it."

"A fox might have got him?" At Derwen, she remembered, foxes were supposed to live in the cliffs, eating cockles on the shore. She was silent, thinking of the forest and the night.

"But perhaps," he suggested, "he's heading for the sea on his own. We'll catch him up on the road, prancing side-ways."

She did not think he really meant this, but for some miles she kept watch for the crab. They had the road to themselves in the early light, except once when a lorry loomed up ahead, drawing a huge trailer. Ralph stopped to let it pass; then another and another. On the trailer sides they read in green and scarlet letters, "Helter-Skelter", "The Haunted House", "The Musical Ride". The three monsters rumbled away into sunrise. Chill air nipped Rowan's fingers and toes. Birdsong rang in her ears. They sped through a sleeping town and out on to open heathland, yellow with gorse and flashing with yellowhammers. The sun was up as they crossed into Dorset and turned towards the sea.

Heathland gave way to fields, scattered copses, deep ferny lanes. Rowan scanned each signpost, directing Ralph with a touch or a single word. They passed a sign saying Steeple, a little church on a hill. Now she was singing again, but inwardly, not daring to make a sound —

"At Boom a great yellow star came out to see;
At Duffeld 'twas morning as plain as could be;
And from something church steeple we heard the
*   half chime,*
So Joris broke silence with, 'Yet there is time!'"

Ralph had been driving with infinite caution, as though in dread of another hold-up, some last-minute mishap. At last came a signpost where he needed no direction. It said, Derwen. Ahead was the grey stone village. Beyond, through a gap in low hills, the horizon brightened. The brightness must be the sea: Derwen bay. Rowan was chanting to herself:

"The broad sun above laughed a pitiless laugh,
'Neath our feet broke the brittle . . . bright
*   stubble . . . like chaff,*
Till over by Dalhelm a dome-spire sprang white,
And 'Gallop' gasped Joris, 'for Aix is in sight!'"

Once through the village, on the flat road between fields, he drove at top speed. Hedgerows went whirling past. Nearly there, nearly there.

The low hedge on their left was dotted with thickets of blackthorn. As they took a bend, Rowan saw a broken thorny branch in the road ahead. Ralph, with the sun in his eyes, swerved a moment too late to avoid it. The front wheel went crashing through a maze of thorny twigs. He never saw the adder until both wheels had passed over its tail. It writhed hideously, streaked for the hedge and vanished. He was off the saddle, rolling back his trouser leg, staring at a small red pinpoint mark in the calf. A spot of blood oozed out. There were scratches on his ankle, thorns caught in his sock. He began to pick them out one by one, bent again to examine the red pinprick, looked up to meet a shocked expression in Rowan's eyes.

"Oh Ralph — were you bit?"

She felt a pang of horror and sickness. She could not stir. He said rather breathlessly, "I *think* it was a thorn. I think so. How do I know?"

He'll know in a minute, she thought. He'll start to swell. She remembered warnings from last year. *They like to lie out in the road. They like the morning sun. You mustn't get bitten in spring, they're brimfull of poison from the winter.*

"Ralph, quick, turn back. The hospital — they keep stuff there for snake bites. Hurry!" His look of fury stopped her. He swung back on to the bike.

They passed the new coastguard house. The old cottage was just ahead. He dashed through the garden.

She saw a note fluttering, pinned to the door: that meant Aunt Lizard was out. Then he was back — "Gone to the cove, it says. Come on. You lead."

She led up a steep slope where they had to grasp at hanks of long wet grass to keep from falling back. They came out on the cliff top, gasping for breath. The sea glittered far below. They jumped over deep cracks as they ran. Something black and glossy on the turf brought her up with a sick jerk; not an adder, a great slug. Ahead was the narrow track to the cove, running down a deep cleft where steps were cut in the turf.

Out on the headland, as though watered by underground springs, wild flowers spilled down to the rocks below; a hanging garden, lemon, pink, blue, purple, emerald: wild mustard, campions, ragged robins, blue-bells, bugloss, hart's-tongue ferns, brilliant against the shining sea, the bank of slate-blue clouds driving in from the west. Gulls hovered in the air like white butterflies, white butterflies blew about like seagulls.

On her visit in July there had been no garden, only grass and harebells. Gazing in astonishment, she collided with Ralph. He had stopped running, he stood at the top of the path, looking out to sea. She heard a low throbbing sound that seemed to come out of the storm cloud. It grew louder. She saw a small white aircraft. Not a plane. It had a kind of windmill twirling on it. She had never seen one before, but she knew it from pictures in Ralph's books: a helicopter.

She watched as it dipped towards them, white paint gleaming. It hung in the air just above them. It was

129

going to crash. She heard Ralph say, "Oh no. Oh no." He was running headlong down the track, calling Aunt Lizard. His voice sounded hoarse, he was so out of breath. In that din Liz would never hear, even if he could find her. Slithering after him, Rowan saw her aunt's grey cat, Cuckoo, crouching by the path, ears flattened, looking up in terror at the helicopter. The noise was ear-splitting.

But all at once it had ceased to hover. It was soaring safely away, out to sea again, buzzing like an insect in the hazy air. The sound died away, and it was gone. In the silence they looked down and saw Aunt Lizard.

CHAPTER
ELEVEN

She was sitting on a camp stool, her back to the pathway, painting the wild garden.

Ralph called. She glanced round, saw them, looked again and started to her feet. Ralph did not move. It was Rowan who scrambled down the last slope, screaming, "Come quick! An adder bit him." She ran back to drag Ralph with her, to show his wound, but he was still standing there. He had picked up the cat and was stroking and teasing him, as though a snake bite were nothing.

Back in the cottage, Aunt Lizard scanned the pinprick and questioned him repeatedly. There was no swelling yet. "You think it might have been a thorn? Well, let's be on the safe side. I shall run you to the hospital." He laughed, he would not go. He threw himself on to a couch, still holding the cat, picking burrs out of Cuckoo's fur with an air of flippant unconcern.

Yet he still looked white and strained. Aunt Lizard came back from the kitchen with a glass.

"Ralph. Be serious. Are you sure you feel all right?"

He grinned up at her. "I feel *extraordinary*. Oh Liz, such a dance you led us. All round the moon. And we came bearing gifts, like the kings of Tarshish and the isles. A cake, and a crab, and strawberries, and a honeycomb. But they all got lost on the way. What's this, snake root?"

"A drop of brandy. Drink it, child."

He sipped, gasped, and tears came into his eyes. Between laughing and choking he got out, "That's right, pour down my throat your last measure of wine — 'Which the burgesses voted, by common consent, Was no more than his due who brought good news' — good news —" He stopped, staring up at Lizard, then added, "There never was any, you know. No news — or good news. It was all a hoax, by R. Browning."

She sat down and looked at him. "Suppose you explain."

There was a long silence. He said at last, yawning, "Telegrams."

"What?"

"Telegrams, there'll have to be. And anger, I shouldn't wonder. To school, and Aunt Em, and — Liz, *you* sent me a telegram. Come at once, it said. Urgent, it said. Honestly. Or am I mixing you up with Lesley?"

Far away came a long low rumble of thunder, then another that seemed to shake the cottage. Rowan thought, Oh, I'll leave him to explain, if he *can*. I'll fetch Aunt Lizard's painting things.

Out in the garden, sheltered from the sea wind, the heat was stifling. The dark clouds had come nearer. At the top of the slope she hesitated. Lightning darted and flickered in the west. She did not want to be caught up here in the storm, alone; but unless she hurried it

132

would be too late, the rain would come, the picture would be spoilt. Eyes shut against the lightning, tripping over cracks and crevices, she made a blindfold dash along the cliff.

But as she ran it seemed to her that already she was too late. The picture would never be found. She would not find the butterflies or the wild garden. What they had heard was not thunder but a landslide. Above the cove the headland had crumbled, toppled and fallen, roaring down to engulf the rocks where Aunt Lizard had sat. When she opened her eyes again, Rowan knew what she would see: a great mound of shale and raw earth, scattered over with flowers like a new grave.

II

A WIND OF AUTUMN

CHAPTER
ONE

"Well, I did see that," said Rowan. "A cliff fall — a land-slide — just where she'd been painting. Only, it was three months later."

"But was your aunt . . . ?"

"She wasn't hurt — she wasn't there. Not when it happened. A lot of people were, though. Down on the beach. Buried alive — one woman was killed. It was all in the papers."

"You saw it *happen?*"

"No, no, Lizzie and I were away in the town. We heard all sorts of sirens, and police and coastguards and ambulances, we thought it was another lifeboat call. But I went up there on the cliff when it was all over. Next day. And then I remembered."

Respectful silence. Rowan added thoughtfully, "In Ireland, if you dream something and it happens — they say, 'There's your dream out'. So people *must* always have known about this? Time, I mean — working backwards?"

"I don't think he quite means that —"

"But Rowan didn't *dream* it, did she? Not asleep —"

"Why shouldn't daydreams count, though?"

"And, look, he says —"

The voice of the shy librarian made itself heard from her corner. "I must ask you to go outside if you want to talk, The library is for silent study."

Dare protested, "Oh, Florence. That means chat, doesn't it? Not a proper debate about Dunne or Donne?"

"You know the rule, Dare. You agreed to it, all of you, when you got your badge."

Each of the girls round the long table wore pinned to her dark red pullover a round gilt brooch the size of a florin, with a design of a Viking ship: the new badge giving entry to the school library, sign of privilege and scholarly intentions. The legend *Quest* round the lower rim had evoked a certain amount of schoolgirl ribaldry, but no one wanted to lose it. For the next ten minutes there was silence, except for the whisper of the wood fire, rustle of pages, the sound of far-off singing from the music room.

Rowan was thankful. She had told that story on impulse, and regretted it at once. Some things should never be told. She had never spoken of it before, even to Ralph. But that had been the beginning — that journey six years ago. And today was the end.

Faint voices sang:

A ship there is, and she sails the sea.
She's loaded deep as deep can be . . .

Rowan shivered. She tried to shut out the singing, to concentrate on notes for her English essay. She found herself reading:

138

... the youth who daily farther from the east
Must travel, still is Nature's priest,
And by the vision splendid
Is on his way attended ...

It was so apt, she could not help smiling. But at this
moment the plane was over the Atlantic, flying west to
America. She was alone, the future empty. Nothing
would ever be the same again. So think of something
else, think of Wordsworth. The little boy out on the hills
in the autumn nights, "scudding from snare to snare
which he had set for woodcocks." The young man in
Milton's room at Cambridge, "dizzy with the fumes of
wine". This morning Dare had quoted the line about
the "old half-witted sheep", and Miss Hereward had
looked for a moment as though she might slap her.
Then she had said courteously, "As you grow older
you'll find, I think, that Wordsworth's poetry will
increase in value for you, and Shelley's will decline ..."
Innocent old Hereward: as though no life would ever be
lived without poetry. But her own grandmother, she
realized, was much given to quoting old ballads; and
her father still read the poets of his youth, those
old-fashioned moderns who used to write about islands
and pylons and bombing raids, and who seemed now
far more out of date than *To Jane, With A Guitar*, or
almost anything else in Shelley. And she'd always liked
it herself — too much, nowadays, for the good of her
G.C.E. prospects in other directions.

A bell. She would be safe now. The others would
have forgotten her story.

All but Dare. Slapping papers, folders, *An Experiment In Time* together, Dare turned to ask, "So what about Ralph? Go on?"

"Ralph?" Rowan tried an absent tone.

Dare looked at her sharply. "He wasn't bitten, I suppose?"

"Oh, I see — oh, no. He was all right too."

Pretending to be lost in reverie, she knew Dare's eye was still on her: "I suppose you know he's on television tonight?"

"He can't be. This minute, he's flying to America."

"Don't be dim. Are you going to watch?"

"Oh, that water vole film *again*! He wasn't *in* it, you know."

"He did the commentary. There's a picture of him and Jeremy Manson — here, look . . ."

Rowan glanced and said languidly, "How can I watch? No television. Besides, boring old Nature — we get enough of that when he's here."

"Did you say America? I thought it was New Zealand he was going to?"

"Yes, and he's going to California first. To see his father and Lizzie. My people have gone too, did I tell you? For a month, nearly."

Dare took this in. "You mean you're on your own?"

"Well, a woman's coming in to sleep." Supposed to be, she added to herself; for the woman was a sister of Lily's, and as usual they had made their own arrangements.

"Oh! You can give a party! Come on, Rowan. It's a long weekend. Tomorrow, shall we? Or Saturday night?"

"Well — I don't know . . ." She didn't want to be rushed into making plans, to break up the marvellous stretch of days, four days, that only came twice a term. She had a month's pocket money. Tomorrow she would go away somewhere — to the races perhaps. Besides — how could one know, now, if one would want a party on Saturday night? Two days ahead?

She tried quoting Aunt Lizard: "Parties bore me rather. What I like is two or three people talking shop in a pub. Gamekeepers, or barristers —"

Dare's blue eyes stared, cold as a Siamese kitten's. "Do you know what Tallis said about you?"

Don't tell me, don't.

"He said" — relentlessly — "about you staying that night in school last term —"

"For God's sake, Dare! If that gets back to the head I'll have to leave."

"Why? If it wasn't breaking rules?"

"Oh, you know what she'd say. 'If five hundred girls all hid in the art cupboard to see what the school was like at night' —"

Dare giggled. "You can say you were being an adventuress."

"'Be adventurous', she *said*." Presenting their *Quest* badges, the head had made a dashing little speech.

"Isn't that the same?"

"Yes, I expect so." Had she escaped the terrible verdict of Tallis? She had not.

"Well. I told him that, and he said — you sounded more like a man than a girl."

"Is that all!"

"Not very flattering I should think."

"From a man it is." But that was only bravado. It was Dare who was the authority on men. At Rowan's home she had once met Ralph and his friend, Jeremy Manson, and saw no reason why this should not happen again. (But his post in New Zealand was for three years. She did not know that yet.)

"Well, come round after tea if you like. We can see the film," Dare offered.

Rowan hesitated. Dare was half out of the door, crying, "I must rush." Roger would be waiting. And probably Neil and David as well. She called back, "Ring later, shall I, anyway? About the party —"

"I might be out, though."

"I'll ring you," said Dare.

The crowd of grey coats and mulberry blazers began surging past the window towards the station. Rowan prepared to put in time.

Last term she had found herself to her dismay a "train prefect", supposed to keep an eye on the younger ones and check any rowdy behaviour. Boys on the train would have outbreaks of fighting and leapfrog; girls were rarely as rowdy as that, but there were other ways of getting on grown-up nerves. The idea, perhaps, was that seniors must learn authority and tact. Rowan thought, however, that the world was full of competent women who enjoyed giving orders — one less would not be missed. She had begun to take later trains to and from school, missing assembly and prayers in the morning. For a whole term this seemed to go unnoticed, the Church of England staff assuming that she prayed with the Catholics, and vice versa: an interesting discovery. But this term the headmistress, with little to learn about tact or authority, had started a new system: the daily lesson at prayers was to be read for a week at a time by one of the seniors. It seemed to Rowan hard luck that she should have been picked as one of the first readers; if she cut prayers now, there would be questions. But in the afternoon she could make a detour through quiet suburban roads, waiting for the grey coats to disperse, before catching a train.

The October afternoon was still and brilliant, with scents of late roses and burning leaves. Great thunder peaks, snow-white and apricot, stood up in the wide pale sky over low-built houses, groves and gardens. In Chestnut Avenue the withered fans had been swept into long wind-rows. Children scuffled after conkers. Sticks and stones, yellow husks, glossy nuts lay strewn about. In Almond Close she picked up a grey-green almond shuck, pale pink inside like a seashell, like almond blossom. What a lot had happened since last spring: a lifetime of feeling and experience. She wandered on, moving in time to remembered singing.

A ship there is, and she sails the sea.
She's loaded deep as deep can be.
But not so deep as the love I am in.
I know not if I sink of swim.

CHAPTER
TWO

Rowan, like all her friends, had been warned, "Never talk to a strange man on the train," and in practice amended it to ". . . *after* he starts pinching your knee". No danger of that with her neighbour this evening. As soon as she opened her library book he leaned slightly to look at it with interest, adjusting his glasses. Looking up, she met a reassuring glance: an elderly don? He said simply, "Photographs by Lewis Carroll?" She nodded and moved the book nearer. In friendly silence they went on looking together: Tennyson's dark furrowed face; little Hallam in tunic and frilly drawers, docile, a shade anxious — it was no joke to be the laureate's child; two upright ladies playing chess; strong-featured serious little girls; a young servant with a beautiful face, rough hands, clumsy boots, no Christian name . . . That brought them to Gloucester Road station. Parting, they smiled at each other. They had not exchanged a word, she was sure they would never meet again. Yet of all the hundreds on the train, he was probably the only other one who would have recognized the photographs. And she had sat next to him! The coincidence seemed delightful.

144

She had to face another that was not delightful at all. Colonel Anson. As she ran upstairs, she heard his cough. He would be hovering on the landing outside his flat, a mournful old Sealyham nowadays, waiting to ask, "How are the studies progressing?" She slowed up, searching in panic for something to answer this time. An idiotic question. The meeting must be as embarrassing to him as to her; yet even when she made some warning noise — slamming the front door, dropping a book in the hall — he had not the sense to escape. There he would be, just coming out or just going in. She resigned herself, turned the corner of the stair and dashed up the second flight. "How are the studies progressing?"

Even in the flurry of departure her mother had found time to put up the winter curtains in Rowan's bedroom, to fill her Chinese bowl with fruit and hazel nuts, to buy flowers and leave the whole flat in beautiful order. This rapidly became less beautiful as she ran from room to room, fetching in dripping primrose plants — brought over last month from Nine Wells for Lesley — off the balcony; mixing bread and milk for the garden hedgehog; finding sugar lumps for the dairy ponies in the stable near the river. There would have to be a day of reckoning before they came back. Perhaps Bridie would help tidy up? But Bridie, Lily's young sister, a probationer nurse, was more likely to spend her spare time anointing her feet and describing operations.

A note on the dresser reminded — "Cold chicken in fridge", and under this, "Don't forget tea!" She was expected at Aunt Lizard's studio, to see her new tenants, the Blacks. Lesley and her daughter, Tabby.

When she arrived a dozen small children were playing on the cobbled strip between the studios; a game with a great deal of running and calling, catching and shrieking. Rowan watched for a moment, remembering autumn days when she had joined a gang after school for bicycle touch and doorbell ringing. She found herself envying the players, as she used to envy the racing scuffling boys in the train. She remembered the excitement, the illusion of risk and outlawry, the sense of timeless evening.

She went slowly up the stairs, rather shy now of meeting Lesley after so long. The last time was that Whit Sunday six years ago, when she was still married to Denys. The odd brief marriage had ended soon after. Tabby was born, and Lesley took her to live in Cornwall, then with an artist's family in France; then for the past six months at Gray Gavine, a country house open to the public, where Lesley had a summer job. She had begun as gatekeeper, then got herself transferred to the gardens. Now Tabby had started school, and Lesley was a designer with a fabric firm near Sloane Square. A long time. They must both have changed a great deal.

As much as *this*? For a moment Rowan stared in dismay at a slight pale woman who sat knitting by the studio window. Then she realized that Lesley was still out at work, and this was someone "minding" Tabby. The little fair girl at her side held a toy sunshade. She was trying to poke at a cat perched in the ash tree; not

Cuckoo nor Apricot, whose race was run, but a young tabby cat that Rowan had not seen before. She looked at the child with lively curiosity. It gave her a cool appraising look in return, then announced, "Tomorrow I'm going to bring my dog, he's very good at killing cats." Small white teeth snapped like a ferret's. The knitter said mechanically, "You know what you'll get in a minute," and to Rowan, "We'll be on our way, if you're staying. Come on then, Deirdre." Rowan saw them go with relief. Tabby must be one of those children outside.

She leaned out. Now the cobbles were in deep shadow. The game had changed. Half a dozen of them were bunched together behind the tallest girl, who looked about seven years old. Another faced her alone. The dialogue came up clearly:

"You can't come in, your shoes are dirty."

"Then I'll take them off."

"No, your stockin's are too dirty."

"Then I'll take them off."

"Feet are too dirty."

"I'll chop them off."

"No, the blood'll run over my nice new carpet."

"I'll wrap them up in a thousand blankets."

"Then you may come in."

The persistent one, triumphant, began to call her children by name. One by one, with shrill cries of terror and relief, they escaped to her. Over Rowan's shoulder Lesley laughed. "'The witch and the mother' — gruesome, isn't it? Tabby brought it back from Dorset. They always start that when it's getting dark."

147

It was Lesley this time; indefinably changed, yet seeming after the first moments hardly changed at all from that clear-cut memory of seven years ago, at Packhorse. She switched on the lights and Tabby swooped in like a moth. Tabby was small and brown with straight brown hair striped blonde by the Indian summer; tabby hair, Rowan thought. Lesley and Rowan were talking at once as though they had seen each other every day. At the table in the window, hastily cleared of loose drawings and portfolios, they sat drinking tea and eating soda bread with Dorset butter and quince jelly. They might really have been back at the farm. The jelly had a fresh delicate taste like the smell of primroses. The cat, Tray, sprang in from the tree, raced out of the door, downstairs and up the tree again; round and round in a clowning gallop, spurred on by their attention. Rowan asked, "Why 'Tray'?"

"Tabby called him that. Why, Tabby?" But the little thing held her peace, looking from one to the other as though they spoke Greek. It did not seem possible that she could have been one of those shrieking brats; still less that she could have taught them a long ferocious dialogue. Nor would she talk about school; although Lesley, to encourage her, described her own day in the crowded studio — "like being at a party all day long" — and Rowan answered questions about her own school. Lesley, who had also been there, looked critically at Rowan's uniform, new this term: long dark red skirt and pullover, pink-and-white striped shirt. "Mm. There was something about gym-slips, though. Oh yes, and those black stockings — I'm certain they'll come in again." They laughed, it sounded absurd. Rowan looked at some fashion sketches heaped on the end of the table. One showed a waif in white silk shirt, dark jerkin and tights.

"What's that for — Peter Pan?"

"Oh — Bergner in *As You Like It*, before you were born. But look . . ." Lesley seized a pencil and sketched rapidly; a model in short tunic, long soft boots to the knee like a jockey's, sleeveless jerkin. A fashion for masquerading children, making today's wide skirts and huge coats look dowdy and middle-aged. Yes, Lesley had flair — she might make her mark as a designer. But Aunt Lizard had said, "She'll never really settle down indoors. Her heart's in the country."

Watching her fingers, Rowan thought — If only I could draw. Or do something as well as that. Sixteen next month. She felt the familiar wave of panic.

Lesley went on sketching, glancing now from her paper to Rowan and back again. Rowan saw a tall skinny girl, long untidy hair, shadowed eyes, bony face; not quite plain, yet with a fleeting elating look of her own face in the glass. Lesley said gently, "It's just a touch of colour you need. You're lucky, you know. Make-up was ghastly before the war. Sticky lipstick like poster paint. Eye stuff like tar. You can't imagine."

"Oh, it's easy to say we're lucky. Mother's always telling me." You girls can take up any profession you like. You're so lucky! But suppose one wanted . . . nothing like that? To be like Lesley herself: not always shut up in classrooms with some new test looming ahead, G.C.E., Advanced Levels, degrees and diplomas.

Suppose you wanted to find some level of your own; or just to explore, or do nothing for a bit? She could not say any of this; but Lesley murmured without looking up, "You sound like the Cockney girl on holiday — 'Thank God I'm shut o' that lot.'"

"It's more, they'll like a rest from *me*," Rowan said with gloom.

"Poor parents." She looked across at Tabby, playing out of earshot, and added, "Sometimes she seems so grown-up, more like fifteen than five, I feel she was *born* knowing more than I do. But then she comes in crying . . . she's seen a cat run over, or some other child's been beastly — and you think — they're on their own already, with all that coming to them. Poor little toads. Helpless, you feel — you wait, you'll see." Subtle flattery again: how could one help liking it?

Running Tabby's bath in the kitchen sink, Lesley found the primrose plants and began talking about the garden in Dorset. She would take the plants there next Sunday while Tabby was at Clare Hall visiting her grandmother: this to the child herself, who appeared suddenly hovering behind them. She began to ply her mother with questions. It was like one of those games, Rowan thought; Lesley answering patiently, lightly, as though each line were familiar. "You're not going out, are you? Do I go to school again tomorrow? When do I go to Granny's?"

"Not till Saturday."

"And sleep there — shall I?"

"One night, yes. Like last time."

"And you'll sleep at that cottage?"

"Merren McKay's, yes."

"And on Sunday you'll come and get me?"

The dark eyes were fixed on her as though asking: Are you sure? Tabby swung from the door by her free hand, clutching Tray in the crook of her arm. The cat was dressed in a doll's bonnet and nightgown. He hung limp, without protest, like a glove puppet. Lesley's back was turned, she was busy with taps and towels; under the rush of water Rowan caught the next whisper: "Gran says — if I lived with her — I could have a pony." A bit ominous? How would Lesley cope with that? Her own mother, Rowan knew, had once felt guilty about bringing her back to London. But Lesley didn't seem to have heard. Perhaps at the moment that was her way of coping.

Rowan had a quick vision of something Tabby would never see: the nursery in the farmhouse cottage, the seascape on the wall. Just in time she bit back a childish, unforgivable "Do you remember?" — and turned away to roam about, looking at their possessions: toys and books, a shabby red velvet rabbit, a beautiful pasteboard Easter egg, pale green, with a golden pheasant printed on it and beads spilling out; a little blue jug with a shiny brown rim; a water colour of a summerhouse in a garden; a high white screen painted with brown and pink moths; baskets of apples, walnuts and corn cobs, a string of russet onions, a toy violin, a dish of flowering autumn crocuses.

On Tabby's bunk she found a child's paper, the *Robin*. Years since she'd seen one of those. She looked through it from cover to cover; then at a new book,

Period Piece, open at a picture: a little girl dressed like one of Lewis Carroll's, on a Victorian sofa. The caption said: "Mrs. Bewick".

Bewick? Aunt Lizard had had a book of old engravings — had she taken it away? No, it was still on the shelf. Rowan looked again with pleasure at the Deer, the Greyhound Fox, the Hare; and then at a graveyard under a sinking moon, the message on the leaning tombstone: "Good Times — & Bad Times — & all Times — get over". A grave forgotten, long grass waving over the past away.

She closed the book slowly. Oh yes, today was one of the bad times; but it would go over. Tomorrow she would feel better. And Lesley was pouring drinks, hot milk for Tabby and Tray, red wine for herself and Rowan. It was sharp-tasting, like sloes or elderberries — could it be? — but the feeling of dizziness and warmth was comforting.

When she left, Tabby was already asleep behind the screen, Lesley curled blissfully barefoot on her divan with bread, wine and Mrs. Bewick. No more work till tomorrow, and then a job like a party. No piles of prep, English essay, history, French, no Reproductive Organs of the Rabbit.

Perhaps envy showed in her face. Lesley whispered, "Do stay if you like? If you won't be too bored?" But it was time to go. Nearly time to see the film — the third showing, the third time; unwise or not, she must see it.

Back at home she hurried out of school clothes into tidy anonymous slacks and sweater. Five minutes' quick walking brought her to streets honeycombed with private hotels. She chose a new one and walked in calmly, a girl staying here, just back from posting a letter. Passing the empty reception desk without a glance, she scanned the glass-fronted "lounge", then walked sedately upstairs. Here it was: a door marked Television Room. She slipped into darkness and found an empty chair. No one looked round. Her heart was bumping, she pressed her damp hands on her knees and tried to breathe naturally. It felt like travelling without a ticket. Could one be arrested for trespass? But this was the only way. There was nowhere, so far as she knew, where one could pay to see television.

Now it was starting. At once the fright and risk were nothing. For this half-hour she was back by the vole river in the happy summer days; when year after year, in school holidays, college vacations, on leave from the Navy, slowly and patiently, Jeremy and Ralph had built up their "documentary": a labour of love. Often she had gone too: a reward for taking their telephone messages, forwarding letters, typing notes for them on Father's typewriter.

Sometimes Jeremy Manson had brought one or two of his pupils. So long as one kept quiet, the voles didn't seem to be disturbed by watchers. By the river, silence was the rule; away from it, the boys were either shy and awkward, almost hostile, or self-possessed and talkative. She was never sure which she found more terrifying. Both kinds, she thought, were less interested in animals than in the techniques of filming. Even the shy ones, given half a chance, could chatter learnedly about gauges, speeds, lenses and different makes of camera. No amount of note-typing would ever improve her grasp of all this. But nothing could have spoilt those days, the beauty of the water meadows, the sense of secrecy and privilege; the tension and excitement of waiting hour after hour for a vital shot; the wonderful pleasure of sharing success, or even sharing disappointment.

Now, as the film drew near its end, she remembered the last time Jeremy had come to the flat; and how, surprisingly, he had talked about the film with misgivings, as though regretting its success, even wishing they had never allowed it to be shown, except perhaps to naturalists.

Once, he said, he had visited a colony of water voles on a river that was thronged all summer with punts and rowing boats. The little short-sighted creatures would swim and dive right under a boat, or sit preening and feeding a few feet from passing oars. Soon he stopped watching the voles and began to watch the people instead. Then he noticed a curious thing. A few of the boaters saw them at once, smiled and pointed them out to each other. A few others might catch sight of one as it dived, and cry, "Ugh, look, a rat." But to the rest, the great majority, they seemed invisible. These people didn't expect or want to see them, and they did not. Now — in letting the film be shown — were they perhaps destroying a safety curtain? Exposing them, not to the risk of casual cruelty — that was nothing new — but, far worse, to loss of peace and privacy? Mass awareness might, after all, be far more dangerous than the reverse.

She had forgotten that till now; but for a moment his anxiety blurred the screen for her like a passing car. She scanned the faces round her in the bluish light. Suppose all these people came flocking to Sussex, searching for the river, trampling the quiet fields, cramming the green lane with cars?

Elderly placid faces, mostly. Several were gossiping — not about water voles. A young Indian woman gazed serenely; two beautiful silent children leaned by her side in a trance of boredom. A fidgety man jumped up again to interfere with the set, and his neighbour snapped at him. Rowan did not think the voles had much to fear from them.

CHAPTER
THREE

She came out into a mysterious London night with mist in the air, a haunting scent of chrysanthemums, leafy plane trees yellow in lamplight, white clouds drifting over a slate-blue sky. Turning into a narrow street, she saw an odd dark hump on the pavement ahead. It broke up into a ring of crouching children — they scattered at her approach. Warily she crossed the road, making a wide detour round that spot. As she drew level with it, there was a muffled explosion under a manhole. Squeaks of laughter came from the shadows, then a thud of footsteps speeding away.

Inside the front hall, she heard a telephone ringing. Half-way upstairs, she realized it was in her own flat. Father and Mother, from New York! She fumbled for the keyhole, flung herself in, then paused and picked up the receiver gingerly, ready to cut off Dare with an *au-pair* girl shriek — "Is wrong numb*air*".

A voice asked "Could I speak to Rowan Dane, please?"

Not Dare. A boy's voice. No one she knew?

"Oh — yes."

"Hello — are you there? May I speak —"

"Yes. Yes, it's me."

"Oh. Well. It's — this is Aldenbury."

Ralph's old school, where Jeremy taught. A message from Jeremy? The voice sounded hoarse and deep, with a note of worry in it. It stopped, she thought there was muffled talk at the other end; then another voice took over, younger-sounding but quite at ease, not anxious at all.

"Good evening. That's Rowan Dane, isn't it? Ralph Oliver's cousin?"

"Yes. Yes, it is."

"My name's Robin Hicks. You won't remember me. But we met once down in Sussex. By the plashy fen, you know." That was Jeremy's code name for the vole river, borrowed from *Scoop*. The voice dashed on — "Awfully sorry to bother you. The thing is — two of us — we're in a bit of a fix." A pause. The voice went a little higher and faster. "Jeremy took us down there this afternoon, me and Johnson — and — we were going again on Saturday. But now we can't. So we just wondered — I thought I'd ask — if *you'll* be there by any chance? If you could help us?"

She waited.

"Hallo?"

"Yes — I'm here. I'm — what did you want me to do?"

"You think you might — this Saturday?"

She said slowly, "I could go tomorrow. I might be going anyway. But —"

"I say, could you really? That's marvellous. Well, look — you know about the pigeon-hole. The place we called —"

She interrupted, "The pigeon-hole and the locker? Yes, of course!"

"Well, the fact is — we've left something there, by accident, in the pigeon-hole. Now we can't go back on Saturday. It's terribly urgent. Someone *must* go. Could you help us?"

"But what is it? What do I do?"

"It's just — something in the pigeon-hole. You'll know when you see it. So you'll go?" And suddenly the airy note was missing. Strain showed through, and tense anxiety.

Uppermost in her mind was distrust, the thought of some hoax or booby-trap, of the rocking manhole cover. She said, "But if it's urgent as all that — *why* don't you go yourself? If it's just cutting some match . . . ?"

She heard her own voice, more waspish than she meant. He sounded taken aback.

"It's not, nothing like that. It's — some of the chaps have started having stiff necks, and temperatures, and so on. So now we're all in quarantine. *You* know . . ."

She did know. A polio scare. They seemed to come every year in the autumn term.

"Well . . . all right. But what *is* it? Do I post it on to you?"

"No, no, no. Just *throw it away.*"

"It's — not some sort of joke, is it?"

"Please don't think that. Do go — will you? You'll know when you see it — and, I say, we'll pay you back of course, train fare and all that. Hello? Are you there?"

"Yes. Well. All right." Of course she would have to go now, or be eaten up with curiosity. Had they counted on that? "I'll be there tomorrow. And I'm to find something in the pigeon-hole, and throw it away?"

"Yes, but look — you won't tell Manson, will you? He'd be so wild. He'd never take us there again. And I'll ring tomorrow night — do you mind? Just to find out? I'm so grateful — I just can't thank you properly . . ." Cheerful and confident again, he talked himself off the line. She put down the telephone, said aloud in the silence, "What effrontery!" and wished she had thought of saying that before.

The telephone rang again. Bridie, checking up, quite ready to be put off. Rowan put her off: "No, don't come tonight — yes, I'm quite all right. Yes, no, I'd rather, see you another time, goodbye." At once there came another ring. New York on the line at last. Her mother's voice, three thousand miles away, five hours back, talking about their flight, then saying the familiar predictable things: "Don't forget . . . Are you sure? . . . Do hope . . . Good night, darling." It sounded very strange, like a message from another world.

Then silence, and the ticking clock.

She looked at the briefcase on the hall floor. Four essays! But it was long weekend, she had plenty of time. No school till Tuesday. And she was going to the river, starting at dawn by the first train.

She slept at once, then found herself wide awake in the dark. She pressed her torch — only two o'clock. Hours of night to go yet. Lights shone from a window in a house across the garden. Tree shadows played to and fro on the ceiling, she could hear the faint rustling of leaves from a lime tree: the sound of autumn, when the leaves were crisp and dry. She never heard them at any other season. She lay still, trying to sleep; thought of horses in quiet fields, squirrels curled in dreys; tried counting sheep; then repeating poetry.

Nobis cum semel occidit brevis lux
Nox est perpetua una dormienda . . .

A good motto for dormice; for a Roman dormouse, the Edible Dormouse — one of those labels the creature itself wouldn't care for. A rhyme began to jig in her head:

What's his grouse?
— He's an Edible Mouse.
And who are you?
— I'm a Scilly Shrew.
A Scillier name I never heard
Except perhaps for an Oven Bird . . .

Ralph had told her about dormice; as a child he had seen them often, but he said they seemed to have vanished from Sussex with the red squirrels.

Just lately she had come across a piece about a dormouse — of all unexpected places — in her favourite *Villette*. She switched on her lamp, picked up the book and found the page. The hibernating mouse was compared to a hermit forsaken and forgotten by those he loved. ". . . the frost may get into his heart and never thaw more; when spring comes, a crow or a pie may pick out of the wall only his dormouse-bones."

She took a hazel nut. An earwig scuttled from the husk, and she put it on a dahlia. She cracked the nut and lay back staring at the lamplit flowers; small pink dahlias, michaelmas daisies, blue borage like the clumps by the fig wall at Nine Wells. Closing her eyes, she could smell the autumn garden, the musky scent of fig trees and queer thrilling sweetness of African marigolds and late yellow plums.

Now one might as well face it. At fifteen she had done with love. Wars apart, or polio, she might live another fifty or sixty years. What else was there? She would have to find something, and *soon*.

Always, until this summer, it had been taken for granted that she would help Grandfather with the horses. Now that was changed. Only a month ago Grandfather had said quietly, "Rowan never comes into the stables now." Overhearing, she was shocked; but it was true. For one thing, she had suddenly begun to shoot up — inches taller by the end of the summer term. Not that it mattered. This year the Nine Wells ponies were being shown by Micky Trim, youngest of three brothers who had taken a neighbouring farm. It was all arranged when she arrived, and she didn't mind. But then there was Foxglove, the gentle Connemara mare she had looked on as her own. Foxglove, whom she herself had named, with her wise blond face, freckled with gold like a white foxglove. She was gone, sold behind Rowan's back, shipped off to South America. Grandfather looked a bit troubled about that; but it had been such a good offer — a friend of Jamesy Trim's.

Once she had ridden from morning till night all through the holidays. Now she wanted only to lie in the grass and read, or listen to the radio. Charitable things were said about her out-growing her strength. But then, in savage bursts of energy, she would disappear on long dreaming bicycle rides by herself, to the waterfalls, or into the mountains; once on the spur of the moment to Dublin, twenty miles, to wander about the college where Ralph had spent three years. Returning, she could only say that she had been sightseeing. "But why by yourself — why not all drive in together?" Why not, indeed; impossible to explain. So there she was, a stranger; a weedy moody young creature, no asset to Irish family life, so exacting and competitive; not to be compared to lively Irish girls, all doing well at school, training for jobs or "making a good match", as the old people still said, and a credit to everyone.

Only the nuns in the convent had not changed. On a visit there with her mother they still praised her to her face and called her a lovely girl; giving one, no doubt, something to live up to. Her mother, told how proud she must be, had looked rueful. (And yet — wasn't there a faint gleam of mischief in the grey eye of Sister Mary Emmanuel, once Emmy's school friend Kitty Quinn?) Rowan tried to picture herself years hence in a convent, being visited by Dare. But what about a vocation?

That was her trouble — she had no vocation at all, no bent for anything so far as she could see. And soon, after G.C.E., there would come the arguments and battles, the plans for her to go to a university. She ought to have a counter-plan ready, something she was sure of, as sure as Ralph had been, coming back from that interview in Dublin six years ago, determined to be a zoologist. They'd all taken it well in the end, when he got around at last to telling them. Aunt Lizard had said, "I always knew you'd break away somehow and live in the woods." Now he was off to do research in great forests of New Zealand. For three years, he said; but as far as she was concerned, she knew it was for ever.

Because she had learned from him to walk quietly, Ralph had sometimes told her she would make a good professional spy. That was truer than he knew. For years, in secret, she had been practising a kind of witchcraft, silent, patient, heartfelt, entirely sympathetic. Collecting relics: things far more revealing than nail-clippings or locks of hair. A locked drawer was full of scraps he thought he had thrown away — blotters thickly scribbled with sketches and mirror-writing; drawings, school magazines, folders full of notes, fragments of poems, school essays, jottings and plans, old photographs, newspaper cuttings.

She had one consolation. No one, she was certain, had ever guessed, not even Dare; least of all Ralph himself. Her instinct was to hide; and last term something had happened to make her even more careful. She'd been talking at break one morning with a girl whom she knew slightly, and it had come out that Sarah was living away from home with an older married sister, up at Highgate. All at once Sarah began to tell about her elder brother's friend, Richard, whose parents were dead, and who had come to stay in the family years ago when he was twelve and Sarah seven. From the first they'd all taken for granted that she was devoted to him — her mother would say to friends, "Of course Sarah *adores* Richard." She did, and he had always been amiable when he happened to notice her. Now he and her brother were both at the London School of Economics. Of course they were often on the telephone to girl friends. Then one day her small brother had said, "Poor Sarah, Richard's thrown her over." Someone laughed; the others had taken it up. Rowan would never forget her companion's despairing voice: "I swear I'd never been a nuisance, never embarrassed him or anything. He liked me, I'm certain. But now it's all spoilt. I had to get away."

Away at fourteen? "But — did they let you?"

She answered, still in that flat little voice, "I didn't ask them. I just went to Caroline's. I'm not going back."

"And your sister — she doesn't mind?"

"It was her idea. She came in one day, they were all making jokes about Richard and me. She saw how it was — she just said, 'You'd better leave, hadn't you,' and I did." Not for the first time, Rowan wished she had a sister. Who else would have thought such feelings mattered?

After a silence she asked, "Do you think — perhaps when you're older — you'll ever see him again?"

No answer. Beautiful dark Sarah smiled to herself, with a look of pride and confidence. So that was it. She was biding her time, and rightly. But Rowan had no illusions of that sort herself. She saw too, with terror, how easily she might have become a victim to that sort of casual teasing.

The danger was over now. It was *all* over — nothing left but her childish collection, and she must burn that some time soon, though not just yet. The hopeless love would go on, absorbing most of her thoughts. She would never get free, never fall in love again, or want to.

No, there was one thing left: the desire for country life, which she and Ralph had always shared. Like Ralph, she must find some way of living there. Not as a zoologist — she would be lucky to get through G.C.E. — but there must be other ways. She would start finding out tomorrow.

One item from the secret drawer she always kept by her bedside for a wakeful night. Tonight she had a file of old papers, some of them in script that must date back to his childhood. Turning them over, she found something she hadn't examined before. Some kind of map, with names she did not know: East Park, Withy Piece, Haunted Lane, and an arrow: To Brookside. It might belong to the time at Beaumarsh; or even earlier, when he and Aunt Lizard had lived for a time in the Forest of Bere. She studied it again, and saw a circle and tiny printed words: Cache tree.

Cache tree! But that tree was on the way to Beaumarsh. She remembered clearly the morning ride from Packhorse Farm to the spring house; the thrush and snail, the beech tree Ralph had shown her beside the lane. The cache was in the first hollow, about

165

twenty feet up — a parcel wrapped in oilskins, put there by himself and two other boys: "Seven years, we said we'd leave it. It's been there two already." Eight years, now. She had asked how they would get it out; quite easy, he said, with a torch and fishing line. He meant to come back one day and do it. But she was sure he never had.

Well, *she* would do it. Tomorrow — today. She would take fishing tackle, take her bike on the train, go to the river first, then on to the lane. She was quite sure she could find the lane and the tree, though this map didn't seem very helpful. What could they have left in the parcel? It would be amusing to find out. She might go on to see Merren McKay.

Then she remembered that she had meant to burn all these papers quite soon; or perhaps seal them up and bury them, like Lucy Snowe with her letters. To find the cache and bring it home would put off that day for a long time, no doubt of that. She would spend — no, *waste* — hours over it, instead of concentrating on her own problem. Perhaps it should be left where it was — and yet, how could she help going, now that she had remembered it?

Well, try the omens; try the Bible. She fetched it, laid it on her quilt, shut her eyes, opened them and the book together: *Their horses also are swifter than leopards, and are more fierce than the evening wolves.* No message there that she could see. Try something else — Shakespeare? . . . *Tongues in trees, books in the running brooks* . . . That was better. The cache was in a tree, the voles were in the running brooks. Try one more. Wordsworth. No, something bigger. *The Oxford Dictionary of Quotations*. She had to find this in the sitting-room bookcase. Shivering, she crouched under a standard lamp and slapped the book open on the carpet . . . *Something hidden. Go and find it . . . Lost, and waiting for you. Go!* She laughed, ran back to bed and fell asleep.

CHAPTER
FOUR

The vole river flowed through lonely water meadows. Mist blotted out sky, woods and downs, all the colours of October. The water ran faster than she remembered, and higher, covering holes in the banks that had been airholes to summer burrows.

She came to the cattle bridge, a low brick archway covered with turf, and looked down into deep clear water streaming with "green hair", crowfoot, cresses, mare's-tail; touched here and there with mauve and yellow, mint and mimulus, china-blue petals of forget-me-not. Willow leaves raced under the bridge. A line of pollarded willow trees stood close to the water, yellow-crowned, trunks twisted into gargoyle shapes, roots clawing at the earth. Others were dotted about the banks.

A moorhen called in the distance. Mist curled and drifted in spiral shapes above the little waterfall. Rooks sailed over, high and silent. There was no sign of life in the weedy stretch of water. The voles must be asleep somewhere out of reach of the floods.

Squelching along the bank, she floundered into a deep hole, soaking her jeans, one sock and the inside of a gum-boot. She thought miserably — I should never have come back; not alone, when we'd been so happy here. But for those wretched boys, I probably wouldn't have. The autumnal chill and sadness merged with her own discomfort into bitter thoughts of Hicks and his accomplice, and this fool's-errand of theirs. It would serve them right if she went away without troubling any more. But she went on, picking her way carefully now among cattle holes, jumping from one clump of rushes to the next.

From the waterside, the willow they called the pigeon-hole looked like all the rest: a leaning trunk with a crown of branches. On the other side the trunk came only halfway like a stable door. Looking in, one saw that the tree was hollow, eaten out at the heart like an apple scoured by wasps. On the inside wall there were useful craggy shelves and pockets, and Jeremy had added a few pegs.

She approached with caution and peered in. At first she could see nothing, then she noticed some object down there on the dark floor. A small wooden box. Stooping over, she was going to pick it up when there was a scuffling slithering noise, and the box seemed to give a jerk. Then she saw what it was: a boxtrap. They must have set it when they arrived, then gone away and forgotten it. No wonder they were worried! It meant chancing that nothing would be caught; or chancing that anything they caught wouldn't starve before they could get there again; or — telling Mr. Manson, and chancing *that*. One could imagine his fury. Patience was one of his strong points, but not with rule-breakers. And that rule was clearly laid down — no box traps without his permission. There were other rules about overnight traps: plenty of bait and bedding to start with. More like a guest-house than a trap, one boy had pointed out, and was advised to shut his guest-house and get on with it.

Well, they were in luck. Whatever they had caught, it was still alive. But what *had* they caught? There was no sound now from down there. She remembered various small fauna, lured, photographed, measured and set free, while the filming was going on. There had been a bank vole, several mice, a shrew. She leaned down to pick up the box, then again retreated without touching it, stood up and shifted from one wet footprint to the other. Hands and feet were icy. She blew on her fingernails and imagined less endearing captives: a rat, an infuriated grass snake? The fishing line had been left in her saddlebag. She wished for strong leather gloves, or some sort of tongs; looked around and remembered the "locker". They might have left something there that would help. Coward! Ah well: no one would know. And if she were brave and got bitten, who would be better off? Well — perhaps Bridie; snake-bite, lockjaw, black plague — she would be delighted.

The locker stood fifty yards away across the meadow, on a daisied lawn that might once have belonged to a cottage garden. The cottage was gone. Now all that remained was this flat strip of turf and a walnut tree, hollowed out like the willow, enclosed in rusty iron bands. As she came near a crow flew away, dropping a blackened husk. Dry curled leaves covered the grass. Inside the tree she found a hank of string and a bunch of rods and poles. She pocketed the string, picked up half a dozen walnuts in their shells, sniffed their bitter scent, then chose a forked stick like a clothes-prop and ran quickly downhill before she could change her mind. She hooked out the trap. It gave a lurch, like a fish on a line. She cried, "Oh!" and dropped it on the grass. The door sprang open, a lively long-tailed field-mouse leapt out, rushed under cover and disappeared. She had an impression of suppleness and grace, a wild bright eye, glossy fur, creamy throat, and wished she could have seen it properly. Anyway, it had come to no harm. From the box she tipped out scraps of grass and rushes, peanuts, a half-gnawed apple. The rules hadn't been flouted altogether.

She wandered down to the waterside. The mist was lifting; faint sunlight showed through. The smell of bruised mint, the last fronds of meadowsweet, the sunlit glittering water brought back an illusion of summer. After all, she decided, she wouldn't hurry away, but have some coffee first, and get warm and dry. She set out across the meadow, past the locker, towards the steep slope of the downs and the distant hanger.

CHAPTER
FIVE

She knew where she was going. She had found it one
June day long ago, coming to look for wild strawberries.
Along the edge of the beeches, among briars and
brambles, she had also found little wild gooseberries
and pink and yellow raspberries, and brought back
handfuls of them in dock leaves. Later there were
hazelnuts, beechnuts and blackberries. But she had said
nothing about the cave. Perhaps no one had ever found
it before.

Yet it wasn't quite like a natural cave. It was a burrow
several feet deep, in a mossy bank at the edge of the
hanger. The roots of a giant beech enclosed it, leaving a
low doorway shaped like a pointed arch. Inside, it was
dry and warm, the chalk walls faced here and there
with flints like a clunch stone wall — someone *must*
have done that, she thought; perhaps a long time ago.
At the back it was high enough for her to stand upright.
The roof was also of chalk, and seemed quite firm. The
floor, hard and dry, was covered with beech leaves. In
the wall at the back was a sort of cupboard like a bread
oven in an ancient cottage.

From the cave one looked out into a ring of hazels,
carpeted with deep green moss. Beyond was a thicket of

briars and spindle trees. In June the bushes had little white briar roses with thick gold stamens. Now hazel and rose leaves were bright yellow, the spindles hung with pink berries. Through this tangle one looked down over green slopes to the vole river shining in the distance.

She drew out an old bucket, blackened by woodsmoke inside and out; one of many finds from a roadside dell two miles away, now a rubbish tip. They had named it the antique shop: useful objects could be snatched sometimes from under the noses of diddycoys on the watch for scrap metal. She lifted a square of moss, planted the bucket and made a fire of dry sticks in it. Over this she placed another find; an iron rod curved in a hoop, like the rods protecting young grass in parks.

The billycan of water, last relic of her wolf cub days, was hung in the middle of the rod, a wet sock beside it, gumboots tilted to steam in the warmth. She made coffee and toasted a sandwich on a hazel stick until drops of cheese oozed out sizzling.

The water meadows lay green and gold in the sun below her. Red bullocks were cropping the grass. She could see the stream ripple and flash, but up here there was not a breath of wind. Beside her, thrust up through grass and moss, was a flat yellow toadstool tied down by blades of grass like bonnet strings. A dead stick was covered in fungus shaped like oyster shells, ringed with fawn and silver. Clematis ropes, tough as ropes in the gym, hung down from a clump in the thicket. Leaning back, crunching the sweet white walnut kernels, she saw gossamers of old-man's-beard against the blue sky. A pigeon cooed somewhere high up; another launched itself, clapped its wings and came gliding down to land a few feet from her and begin turning over the leaves for beechmast. She lay still. Soft pigeon feet plodded over the moss. A robin dashed out of the thicket, sat on a branch and began ticking at her. The pigeon stopped and turned its head about, questing with one brilliant eye, then the other. The robin flirted its tail, fidgeted, sang and vanished. The pigeon cracked another nut. But the fire was sinking. She reached out for a handful of sticks, and the startled bird flew with a rush. One feather floated down.

Now that she must not do: it would give her away to anyone who might be about. Suddenly she knew that she wanted to own the cave, to have it as a refuge to come back to. That idea must have been in her mind all the time. And no one else must find it.

She looked at the doorway under the tree roots, then got up and stooped under them. They made a porch with chinks of light showing through. She could cover them over with branches and moss, hide the entrance completely — then it would all seem like part of the bank, and no one would think of looking for a cave.

All at once she remembered the willow hurdles, bought from a gipsy one rainy month, to make "hard standing" near a boggy patch on the bank, where a family of water voles came to feed. They had found the young gipsy camping in the green lane a mile away, where she had hidden her bike this morning. He had driven a hard bargain for the hurdles; nowadays they

were in demand as garden fences. They noticed he was
wearing dark blue trousers and jersey like a sailor's, and
Ralph — just through his own national service —
thought he too might have been in the Navy, but asked
no questions. Afterwards they had heard by chance that
he was absent without leave and would be put in prison
if he were caught, but they all had a feeling that
wouldn't happen.

Anyway, his willow mats had come in useful. They
used to be stowed away for safe keeping under the
cattle bridge. Could they be there still? She could
wedge them among the beech roots, tie them securely,
thatch them over with moss. She would pull bracken to
hide the doorway, and to make a thick warm carpet
inside. There was the river for water, plenty of firewood,
shops in villages round about. She would have her own
home, like Merren's downland cottage, and come here
often.

She had started downhill to fetch the hurdles when it
struck her that she might be seen carrying them up to
the hanger. No one was in sight, no fisherman,
farmhand or gipsy; local children would be safely in
school. But still it was risky in daylight; that errand
should be done in the dark. Meanwhile she would visit
the cache tree, then buy food and prepare for the first
night in her own home.

She gathered firewood and armfuls of soft brown
bracken from the undergrowth, stored all this in the
cave and set off.

Collecting the bicycle from behind a hedge, she
made her way to a crossroads and up the steep road

behind the hanger, then coasted down the treacherous twisting hill called Diddy-Bone-Snap. Merren said this was short for "Diddycoys' Bones Knap": once supposed to have been a gipsy graveyard. High up to the west lay Merren's cottage, behind new plantations that had replaced the hangers cut in wartime: stands of yellow larch, green fir, beech with hazel, rowan and hawthorn.

At another crossroads she paused for a moment. One road led west along the valley to Fitching village. Straight ahead was the road by which she and Ralph had come that morning long ago. Somewhere along it, past the racing stables, was the lane she remembered, and the tree. That should come first. She rode north.

CHAPTER
SIX

Comma butterflies drowsed on a clump of brambles, flickering their scalloped wings open and shut in the burning noon light. She leaned above the nearest to see the white comma, then the tawny upper side, spread catlike to the sun. She breathed softly on the brown fur of its back, and with a drowsy elegant dip it removed itself to another spray.

Blackberries were mauve, rotten-ripe, thick with basking flies. Ivy flowers were coming into bloom; small brilliant wasps prowled on their dark leaves.

Just ahead was the stretch of road she remembered. Dogwood and maple made a rough hedge between tall straight beeches. Russet leaves strewed the short dry turf; that May morning, there had been dog-violets and a bee orchid. Here and there were sycamore seedlings, pale bright leaves smudged with black like gobbets of soot. Winter wheat already showed faint green in a chalky field over the road. Five dead moles hung on a gate bar, whiskered snouts and pallid paws dangling. A live mole ran across from the ditch, lifted its strange fierce face to the light, drank from a tree-root puddle and ran back.

And she could not find the tree.

She came to a bend with a farm in the distance; turned and went slowly back, scanning each tree again as she came to it. Yes, she was sure this was the place. But on the cache tree there had been a hollow jagged stump, twenty feet up, where years ago a bough had broken off. Another branch grew just above. Ralph said they had thrown a rope over this and swarmed up. She could see nothing like that now. Had the tree fallen, or been cut down?

As she loitered she heard the sound of hooves and saw a boy coming up the farm drive on horseback, a man walking at his side. The rider turned his pony's head to come along the lane. It was a pretty light bay with long mane and tail. He was trying to put it into a trot, while the pony laid its ears back and kept to an obstinate tittuping walk. The man called impatiently, "Well, ride him, then!" At last it broke into a trot, dancing and tossing its head. Now the young rider was trying to hold it in. He was not enjoying himself. As they passed, Rowan heard him muttering "Stop it, you beast, stop it," sounding unnerved and petulant. The pony pretended to shy at a piece of paper in the ditch, backed across the road, swerved round the paper, plunged and set off at a bucking gallop. Perhaps it would settle now; but that didn't seem likely. Like a class of children with a timid teacher, it would probably trot out one trick after another. She sympathized with the boy and then forgot him.

Inside the wood something was crashing about in the hazels; a squirrel, she thought. Grey or red? She had never seen a red one. Ralph said they had lived here

178

once, plentiful as tabby cats, handsome as tortoiseshells. A ride, curving overhead into an arch, ran from the lane into the wood. She wandered along it, but no squirrel appeared. A cock pheasant idled across a clearing, letting the sun warm its back, like the butterflies. The ride was strewn with straw and chaff, pitted like a hen-run with dust baths. Every fifty yards or so she passed a hazel rod, upright in the turf, a white card stuck in its cleft top. She reached the end of the ride and looked over a hedge into a field of tall stubble, swarming with young pheasants.

Standing still, she became aware of stealthy movement all around; pheasants everywhere, in the field, in the wood, creeping into cover. A cock whirred and called. She realized that the hazel sticks might be marks for guns, for a shoot; perhaps tomorrow, perhaps the first of the season. Trespassing in town, in hotels, might be harmless — here, she realized, it would be a felony. Disturbing game before a shoot must rank with "frightening the horses" at Grandfather's. She fled back towards the road, expecting at every turn to meet an angry keeper.

Pausing on the bank to breathe again, she heard hoof-beats coming rapidly nearer. The skittish pony again, still galloping, and slewing about like a riderless horse. It *was* riderless. It dashed past, mane, tail and stirrups flying. At the farm gate it slowed, stopped, then trotted quietly along the drive.

What about the boy? He might be lying somewhere with a broken leg. She walked quickly along the lane. It struck her, after a few hundred yards, that probably a search party would set out from the farm; but no one had passed her yet. She went on.

And now, after a quarter of a mile, she realized that she had come to another stretch of road like the one she had left; beech trees, undergrowth, hazel coppice, greensward. But not exactly like: the road had been widened, the grassy margin cut to a narrow strip, violets and bee orchids swept away. But the beeches were still there. Could she have been mistaken — was *this* really the place she wanted? She began to look out again for a tree with a jagged branch. She had almost forgotten the unlucky rider when suddenly she saw him in the distance.

He seemed to be writhing in agony on the ground. Running forward, she was going to call out when he sat up, then stood up, making brushing movements with his hands as though dusting himself down. So he couldn't be badly hurt. Now he was sitting again, his back to her. She approached silently, meaning to turn back if he seemed all right. Then she went more slowly, staring.

He hadn't heard her coming. He was gathering handfuls of dust and mud, smearing the left side of his coat and breeches. He wasn't brushing himself down. He was deliberately making himself *look* dusty: like someone who had been thrown. And now he seemed quite cheerful, whistling between his teeth. Then she trod on a stick. He looked round and saw her.

For a long moment they stared at each other. If he was filled with confusion, so was she. Both blushed scarlet. He looked at her defiantly, but it was too late

180

for bluff. She thought he might curse her for spying. Then she heard the sound of a speeding car, and darted into the bushes out of sight. A Land Rover came up, braked hard and stopped. The man she had seen at the farm jumped out, calling, "Bobby, are you all right?" The boy hobbled a few plucky steps, gasping, "Nothing much, Uncle — just a bit dizzy. All right in a minute. That little devil — managed to get me off." He was overacting. The man thought so too — he said shortly, "Come off it. Turned him loose, didn't you?" Bobby muttered something, and "Uncle" retorted, "Don't worry, you won't get the chance again." As they drove off, the boy turned his head and shot a venomous look in her direction. Rowan leaned against a tree and giggled. One way or another, he had got his own way, and good luck to him.

She was left alone, but still she didn't move. She found herself looking intently at something close by. The remains of a tree, a burnt-out trunk, six feet high, a silver-grey shell with blackened edges — struck by lightning?

She looked at it, and then at the trees on either side. Had she found what she was searching for? If so, it was too late. She scrambled up to look inside; only thick grey-black ash, shallow rainwater, cigarette cartons.

So that was that. The boys' cache was lost. She would never know what they had hidden. Years ahead, all passion spent, she might ask Ralph himself; but by then he would have forgotten.

CHAPTER
SEVEN

Rowan sat on a bedroom window-sill of pink unpainted wood, looking out through unglazed windows. This new little cottage, not yet finished, smelled of fresh sawdust, distemper and putty. She had found it by following a bridle path from the lane, marked by horses' hooves. It stood just below a spinney of young beeches; the back bedroom window looked straight into the trees, the front on to a paddock where horses grazed. No one was about, and the cottage had no doors yet; she could not resist exploring. Like a toy house, she thought: two rooms up and down, red brick walls, brown-tiled roof, wide windows, staircase with no banisters but a glossy white wood paling. A house for a head groom, or for stable lads? Whoever was going to live here, she envied them.

Down there, the racing stables lay quiet in the sun. Above yellow lichened roofs a wind vane hung without stirring: a copper racehorse stretched at a gallop. There was no wind now. On three sides of the valley were steep gold beech woods; to the south lay the long sweep of downland, Holt Down, Fitching, Alderton, low green hills dark with yews, hiding the weald and the distant sea. On this dreaming afternoon the whole landscape seemed peaceful and still; but, listening, she realized that it was full of sounds — scattered bird cries, goldfinches, travelling martins; hum of tractors; shouts from a potato field where spinner and pickers were working; bursts of metallic hammering and banging down near the village; and more hammering near by, from a house that stood among lawns and trees at the head of the valley. But at school one learned to cut out sounds at will, to think one's own thoughts or swim into a dream . . .

Waking with a jump, she saw that now the sun was in the west. A blackbird swept past, giving its startled evening call. Rabbits swarmed over the downland slopes. Voices floated up the valley; birdlike cries of children out of school. The horses grazed downhill towards the paddock gate. Reluctant to leave this cottage where she had felt so happy, she looked once more into the east room. After the radiance in which she had sat for hours, it looked cool and dim as a crypt. Outside the young beeches stood like candlesticks, shedding a glow that dissolved into mist and shadow along the spinney floor. In winter the full moon would shine down into this room, filling it with black tree silhouettes. Tomorrow, dawn light and early mist would steal through the empty window frame. Why not come back here to sleep? But she remembered the cave. That was hers — here she was trespassing, as usual.

She must go. There were things to be done at once; food to buy; a postcard to be sent to Robin Hicks — that would need thinking about; and a telephone message to Bridie. She wasn't the worrying kind, but one never knew. If tomorrow she were to find the flat empty, Rowan's bed unslept in, she would hope for the worst and might raise Cain. Next time one must leave a gone-to-the-country note.

She picked up her bicycle from the ditch and bumped down the track into the road. As she drew near the large house, a group of workmen came out, put tools and bags in the back of a van, lit cigarettes, climbed in and drove off. A builder's sign hung from a tree; a house agent's board said Fitching Grange, Flats To Let.

Through a gate she could see mossy rosebeds and over-grown creepers. It was like the moated grange:

With blackest moss the flower-plots
Were thickly crusted, one and all . . .

But soon, no doubt, new tenants would change all that; expensive landscape gardeners would take over.

She turned west along the Fitching road. Freewheeling down a slope, she felt a jarring check; the chain had come off, it was trailing in the road. She leaned the bicycle against a field gate and knelt down to struggle with it, her fingers growing black and sticky with oil. Someone darted from a gap in the hedge, lifted the chain on one finger, whirled the pedal expertly, and the thing was done. She looked up at a dark face, a gipsy boy. Over the hedge she saw a crowd of potato pickers at work, women and children. The boy stood smiling. Diddycoy, proud Romany — which? Could one pay him, would he mind? Watching her thoughts, he grinned again and slid away behind the hedge, "with a graceful wave", she thought, "of his slim brown hand". She felt a bit piqued at his self-possession. Seeing a smaller child at the gate, she crossed its palm with a shilling and sped on, making up a shopping list as she went along.

Rationing was over. For the first time in her life, in England, she could go into any shop and buy whatever she needed.

Close to the village she passed Fitching common, fifty acres of rough grass, rabbit holes and gorse. On the far side there was an encampment, with men at work sorting a lorry-load tipped over the grass; bits of old cars, iron pipes, bedsteads, rusty gas stoves — a tinkers' workshop. Scrap metal paid better than potato-picking or willow fences. The cars and caravans drawn up around the tip were new and gleaming, a far cry from the old wooden vans she remembered on Irish roads, drawn by rough-coated horses.

She passed the Manor Farm and its great thatched barn with black beams, supposed to be ancient ship's timbers. Under a low flint wall on either side of the farm gate was a strip of short turf full of wild flowers and snail shells, and there was something delightful about this. In the past, visiting Merren McKay, she had noticed it. One felt that the spot had not changed for centuries, that generations of Fitching children must have collected the little shells; that there had always been clumps of double daffodils there in spring, and then tiny red geraniums, speedwell and primrose-coloured toadflax, right through to winter, as there were now.

The village shop stood by the green. Beside it was a cottage with a tiny bow window showing the name of a great Bank. Next to this was the village hall, an army hut from the first war, corrugated iron painted green, white window frames, a printed poster in a glass case. She read: "Local Government Act 1933. Parish of Fitching with Holt. Notice of Parish Council Meeting. Notice is hereby given that an Extraordinary Meeting of the Fitching with Holt Parish Council will be held in the Village Hall at 6p.m. on Friday October 9th 1953. Subject: Fitching Common. The Meeting will be open to the public unless the Council otherwise direct. Dated this third day of October One thousand nine hundred and 53. Signed John Taplow, Clerk." The date was today's.

They were supposed to have read about parish councils in a book at school. An Extraordinary Meeting sounded extraordinary, like a mad tea-party. But she must hurry, the shop and the post office would be shutting.

Five minutes later she came out, stowing packages into her rucksack and carrying a plain postcard. There was a pencil in her pocket; but what message to send Hicks? It should be cryptic but reassuring. Ten minutes to post-time. She ran across the green and went into the church. No one else was there. She found a Bible and sat down to search feverishly in what seemed a likely spot. Eight minutes later she walked back to post the card, addressed to R. Hicks, Aldenbury, Herts. On the other side she had written: "Ps. 124 v. 7". It was the best she could manage in the time.

CHAPTER
EIGHT

The red post-van arrived. Behind it a bus from Alchester drew up. Women with shopping bags got out, a tall youth, then several boys and girls in school blazers. Two small children, waiting on the green, pounced on the last of these, who looked like brother and sister. The children clutched at the pair, jumping up and down, crying, "Brenda — Barry" — fighting to be first with some piece of news. In breathless staccato, Rowan caught, "Dad's gone to hospital" — "Dad cut his finger off" — "Chopping wood, Jenny jumped on his back" — "Oh, I didn't mean to" — "Only the top, like a thimble" — "Yes, and he picked it up and ran to the doctor, and . . ."

They went off over the green towards the French camp, the older boy and girl hurrying in silence, the other two jumping and piping beside them. The tall youth looked thoughtfully after them.

Rowan went to look again at the parish council notice. *The public will be admitted* . . . should she wait and see what it was like? Merren might be going. If so, she might still be at the schoolhouse. She went back across the green to this small Gothic building. The date 1815 was carved over the door; but nowadays there was an annexe in the field behind, two new classrooms like glass cloches. She knocked at the closed door, then went on to the annexe, tapped again and looked through the glass walls. A cleaner was busy, deafened by her own toil. There was no sign of Merren; she was probably having tea at the Fox and Hounds, as she sometimes did when she worked late.

The inn had a tea-garden, wooden tables and chairs on a patch of grass among fruit trees and staddle stones. It looked green and pleasant in the evening light. A stream ran by the hedge, a tributary of the vole river. No one was there, after all; but Rowan sat down under a pear tree, and presently a woman brought her a tea-tray with boiled eggs, bread and butter, plum jam and canary-yellow cake. Paying for all this at once, she asked about Merren, and was told that the schoolmistress had gone off on the previous bus to Alchester, "with that great cat of hers in a basket. Taking him to the vet, I thought." She turned away to another customer.

The newcomer was the youth who had got off the bus. He sat down at a table some way off, and Rowan ate her eggs, surprised to find how hungry she was. But suddenly he stood up and came wandering over the grass, pausing by her table to say, as though with hesitation, "Did I hear you ask about Merren McKay? Because I saw her in town, with old Badger — going to London for the night, she said."

The woman now appeared with another tray, and planted it firmly on Rowan's table. With a "May I?" so grown-up and charming, it made her think of the Romany boy, he sat down. She was actually having tea with this elegant young man. Like a clever sixth-form boy, he looked, wearing a black fisher-knit jersey with a high collar. He had bright black eyes behind butterfly-shaped glasses with thick gold-coloured frames; dark waving hair, white teeth, fine black eyebrows — even Dare would have been impressed. And of course it was an honour; but she would rather have finished her tea in peace. What could she say to him? Her hands shook a little, she put down her cup with a clatter.

No need to worry, though. Eating and drinking steadily, he took charge of the conversation. She had only to say yes, no, or oh. He was going to this parish meeting. Would Rowan be there? Oh, she would? Was she, by any chance, the *Star*? From Churchfield? He added, "I'm from the *Courier*." Seeing her still at a loss, he added slowly and kindly, "A reporter. From a local paper. The *Courier*, at Alchester."

She stammered, "But — I thought —" He interrupted, laughing, "Oh, I know, I know! You thought I was still at school! I've had this for years, ever since I started. Up north it was, 'Eh, lad, y' don't look old enough to be out reportin'! Come in to fire and get warm!' Exploited, they thought, like an orphan chimney-sweep. Cups of tea, slabs of cake — and they'd tell me anything."

"Up north?" Confused, she was thinking of Ulster.

He said modestly, "Well, Manchester, last year. The *Warden*." But that glory was lost on Rowan. She asked, "Is there — did you mean — you said something about the *Star*?"

"Well, they do send from Churchfield sometimes. This meeting — there's quite a row going on, you know. By the way! Did you say you'd seen Merren lately?"

But she was following another train of thought. Forgetting her shyness, she answered absently, "No, not for ages," and then, "Is there a girl on that paper, though? On the *Star*?"

"I expect so. There usually is."

She nodded and went on stirring her tea with inward triumph. He'd thought she was old enough to be working. How different from Mother's friends, who were always saying, "My dear, she *doesn't* look fifteen!" Not that one wanted to look old, of course — but not *backward*. She asked carefully, "Supposing you — supposing I wanted to live out here in the country — could I earn money like that? On a paper, I mean? If they'd have me?"

For the first time he looked at her attentively.

"You mean, you're coming to live in Fitching?" He sounded quite interested, even approving. Suppose one told the truth? Careful, careful.

"Oh, well. I thought I might. Not in the village exactly." Then recklessly, "What I really want is to live in the woods somewhere. Or out on the downs, in a — a hut, or a cave. But I'd have to get some money somehow."

Now I've done it, she thought. He'll think I'm wrong in the head, or weird, or showing off. She wanted to jump up and rush away. But he astonished her. He said seriously, "I see. Of course, the way to live in the country's to have a job in the country."

"Like a land girl?"

"Not necessarily. You could be our Fitching stringer." He smiled, but added thoughtfully, "Funny your saying that — about wanting to live in the woods, I mean. It's always been an idea of mine." He went on in the friendliest way to talk about it. His best friend at school, he said, had a grandfather who was a gamekeeper in Norfolk. "He had a sort of gipsy caravan in a wood, and we used to camp there in the holidays. I thought I'd live like that, somehow, when I grew up."

Another strange coincidence; like that professor in the train, knowing about the photographs. Or were there, could there be quite a lot of people really who liked the same sort of things? So that one would go on meeting them?

"But do you? Live like that now, I mean?"

"Oh alas, I don't. I don't want to any more. It was just that you reminded me." He took out cigarettes, offered them to her, lit one for himself and continued in that confidential tone, "As a matter of fact, I want to write plays. And they're building a theatre in Alchester — did you know? That's why I came here really. I've done one play already."

"You mean, one that's been *acted*?"

"Well, broadcast. So first I'm going to be the *Courier* theatre critic — they don't know yet — and then . . ." he smiled and leaned back, tilting his chair. He looked younger than ever, despite his ambitions; too young to smoke, or to be on any paper but a school magazine.

The smoke was deep blue against the scarlet pear leaves. Watching it, she wondered — could he be inventing all that? About his job, even? She felt sure he wasn't.

She said, "I did mean it, you know. About wanting to earn some money, and live here somewhere."

"Yes, and why not? You can be a district reporter, and send the stuff by carrier pigeon."

She persisted, "But there wouldn't be anything happening, would there? Not in this quiet little place."

"Well, enough to keep you in cigarettes. News", he added instructively, "doesn't happen only in capital cities."

"No ..." She remembered Derwen cliffs, the Pressmen and cameras after the landslide.

"And one of my editors used to say, wherever you go, the dullest street, the smallest village — there's at least three stories waiting. You've only got to dig a bit."

There was a silence. Then he stood up, saying slowly, "You know, this minute, I think there's something I ought to follow up. Over there." He was looking towards the French camp on the far side of the hedge.

She realized suddenly what he was thinking of: "Oh, those children! They said — their father'd chopped a finger off!"

"Jenny and Primrose. Yes, I heard."

"It sounded awful. Was it true, d'you think?"

"Knowing that family — yes. Yes, I'm afraid it might be."

He added, "I do know them, you see. Quite a saga it's been." He threw his cigarette into the stream, listened for the tiny hiss, then turned back to Rowan: "The thing is — if he's gone to hospital, they're on their own, poor kids. Shall we go and see?"

CHAPTER
NINE

The French camp had changed its role more than once since the day in August 1944 when Aunt Lizard, bicycling past from Beaumarsh, had jumped off on impulse to shake the hand of a soldier at the gate, because of the news that Paris was free: an un-English gesture to which, after a moment's alarm, he had responded with floods of cordiality.

The French soldiers, the workers from Europe were gone now, and the camp was full of families waiting for homes. Vaguely expecting a waste land, bleak and squalid, Rowan was surprised to find lawns and gardens among the concrete squares and rows of Nissen huts. That change, the reporter said, had been started by the whole village, stirred up in the first place by Merren McKay. She had seen with dismay a jungle of weeds and rubbish replacing the vegetable plots kept by some of the "displaced persons". Determined that none of her children should grow up in a rural slum, she had petitioned the parish council, various committees, local farmers and the women's institute. Two elderly men were the first to respond, coming with scythe and billhook to cut down docks and thistles. Then a farmer lent a mechanical cultivator, the village collected seeds and plants, and Merren launched the children on a "nature project", digging up nettle roots and replanting them in a great mass in one corner of the camp; to encourage ladybirds, and tortoiseshell and peacock caterpillars. The children went on to make a hopeful collection of caterpillar plants, cuckoo flowers for orange tips, dog-violets for fritillaries, vetches, thistles, lady's bedstraws; and — more immediately rewarding — ragwort for "cinema" moths. Meanwhile, for "rural studies", a local gardener advised them about clearing the land with a potato crop, then sowing grass and planting herbaceous borders; and a livestock expert went with them to market to choose goats and rabbits.

That was really the starting-point of a village campaign about the gipsy problem. For months at a time gipsies had been camping on the common, where legally they could stay only for one night at a time. Now the idea was that the County Council or Rural Council should be urged to buy land and set up a permanent camp for them, so that gipsy children could go to school — and so that the common should be clear again.

But Merren couldn't wait. She had a gipsy boy due to take his grammar school exam next term, and his sister next year. So she had bought a small paddock near her cottage — part of an old polo-ground, long disused — and had given it to that family, the Fallas.

Telling Rowan about this, the reporter looked at her and added, "I hear there's been a bit of trouble, though . . . ?" and paused, as though waiting for what she would say. When she asked what sort of trouble, he couldn't tell her; only — there were rumours that Merren and the Fallas had had anonymous letters and threats of some kind. From jealousy, perhaps; or just prejudice. "You so often hear people say, 'We don't mind the real Romanys, it's those diddycoys we can't stand.' But the truth is, they don't want *any* of them around."

They had reached the far end of the camp, and he paused in front of a hut. Before he could knock, the door flew open and four bright faces appeared, only to droop at once with disappointment. The tall girl — Brenda? — said dully, "Oh Tony —" and drew the others aside to invite them in.

The long hut was divided into two, the lower end partitioned into bedrooms, the upper forming a kitchen living-room with a tortoise stove, unlit. A pile of firewood and a chopper lay beside it. Rowan looked quickly away, in case of bloodstains. The place felt gloomy enough without seeing those. Electric light burned dimly, flickering now and then. They found seats, and the four went back to their tea-table. Children's Hour from a radio took over in the silence. No one was eating. They were on the alert, listening, but not to *Bluecap and the Singing Wheel*. The voices chattered away in the background, Bluecap the Gnome, the Widow Nettle . . . this wasn't their moment.

Brenda said they had gone to the doctor's house: Father was in hospital, the doctor had taken him there and would drive him back, unless — she stopped. Again there was uneasy silence.

Tony rushed into an account of an inquest he'd just come from; an unfortunate cowman had amused himself in his spare time by dressing up as a nun and pretending to hang himself from a beam in the cowshed, until he went too far . . . half-way through, Tony seemed to realize that the story might not be suitable for such young ears, but Jenny and Primrose sat agog. Barry and Brenda, too, forgot to watch the door with that strained look. Where Children's Hour for once had failed, the inquest had succeeded. Then a car drove up and Barry sprang to the door while the others sat tense, waiting.

The doctor appeared alone; a neat dark woman who began at once, in a voice so soft and quiet that they all had to prick their ears, "Your father's quite all right. Quite comfortable. He sent his love. And the finger's all stitched up. But he won't be home for a day or two, we're keeping him in for a rest." Then, to Barry and Brenda, "Poor Father. Try not to let him get too tired."

She was gone; but the gentle authoritative voice had done its work. Rowan saw the four look at one another; not gleefully at first, but with a long sober look, like a warning against false hopes. Suddenly the light came full on, and in the radiance they were all blinking and laughing with relief, Barry lighting the oil stove, Brenda putting on the kettle, the two youngest inviting Rowan, "Come and see my own room . . ." "And mine . . .". They led her in and out of the partitions, pointing out household treasures, including a tinted photograph of their mother. Rowan saw a pretty young woman, fair-haired, pink-cheeked and smiling. As in other

198

families, the same features had rearranged themselves among the four children with quite different results. They all had that light hair, blue-grey eyes, snub nose and wide mouth, which in Brenda and Barry added up to plain good-humoured faces. Jenny was plain too, but with something vital and engaging they lacked, and which was not in the portrait either. While Primrose — what a risk they'd taken with that name! But it had paid off. She was the beauty, a graceful blonde like her mother.

Rowan wondered how long the mother had been dead; and what it would be like to be Brenda, mistress of a house at thirteen or so. In some ways the idea was not unattractive. Still . . .

Going back to the village, Tony began to tell her about them. The mother wasn't dead after all: skipped, he said, some time ago. The father had been a tractor driver on the manor farm in those days, with a tied cottage; one of several she had seen near the common, old-world, red-tiled, with roses, honeysuckle, a wash-house and a well. But the mother, brought up in town, just couldn't bear country life any longer. She'd been buried alive for years, she said, and she disappeared, leaving the father with four young ones.

Almost at once they all went down with measles. He had to stay at home to nurse them, and he caught it himself and was seriously ill. Next it was chicken-pox. Neighbours and relations were sorry for them and did what they could to help, but they had their own jobs and families. The district nurse was sorry for them, but she could manage only two short daily visits. Attempts

199

to find them a home help came to nothing. The farmer was sorry for them, but he had to have a reliable man. Everyone was sorry, everyone saw they needed help, but it was really no one's business to give it. In the end, the father had notice to quit. No chance of another house, of course, but he found a caravan near Alchester, and a job as a long-distance lorry driver, all he could get just then. That led to more trouble; he was fined for speeding, and driving too long without rest, to get home to the children; at the same time he was "warned" about leaving them alone. In school holidays he took them all off with him in the lorry, and the children loved that, but it was against his employer's rules; again he risked losing his job. He ended in hospital with a breakdown, his family "in care" in four separate foster homes at Alchester, with a promise that as soon as possible they should be together.

"That was where Jenny came in. She's much the brightest, and she's like Merren, can't wait for promises. One day she told her school teacher some tale about going to visit her mother in the afternoon. Then she walked across the town to where Primrose was living, and told the foster mother she had a half-holiday. Then, when the poor woman's back was turned, they ran off to the station and got on a train to Portsmouth, where their mother was. At the other end they slipped through somehow, and walked off to find their mother in the wicked city. So they did, eventually."

"They knew the address?"

"No, but — well, by that time the police in Alchester were after them, with loud-speaker vans, and someone remembered seeing them at the station. So the hunt switched, and they were found on Southsea beach, the seagulls covering them with sand . . . no, no, not exactly. But next day the father told us the whole story, and the nationals used it, with lovely pictures of Jenny and Primrose. And the mother read it and came back to see them. Not to stay of course, she's with another man. Then there was quite a fuss about housing and welfare and Father's gallant struggle. So now he's back on the farm and they've got this hut, and a council house one day, and at least they're all together. And," he finished slowly, "poor devil, he's still so done up, he can't even chop a few sticks without doing himself a mischief."

"So he'd better hurry up and find a new wife?"

"You tell that to Jenny. Quick — we'll be late for the meeting."

She had forgotten the meeting; and had had no idea, really, of going to it. But she found herself inside the hall, sitting with him at a small card-table beside a long board on trestles. Lower down there was a row of chairs for the public. Tony was saying urgently, "Look. Did you say you were staying with Merren?"

Without waiting for an answer he went on, "About those rumours — letters, or whatever — if you hear anything, could you let me know, d'you think? Here, keep this." He turned away to talk to a parish councillor. She was holding a card: "Tony Markwick,

The *Courier*, Alchester", she read, and two telephone numbers. She felt flattered, but puzzled too. It was hard to picture the forthright Merren getting sinister anonymous letters, still less complaining about them if she did. Yet he seemed quite in earnest. She slid the card into her pocket.

The public seats were filling up. No gipsies, she noticed. Tony Markwick came back and pointed out local celebrities: a retired county cricketer, a practising scandal-monger, the Vicar, the "gipsy policeman", so called to distinguish him from the "bee policeman", who knew how to take swarms. This P.C. Watt, he said, knew the gipsies particularly well, because he had to keep visiting them to hand out summonses for camping on the common. "Then they get fined, two pounds a day, and a pound a time for 'depositing litter'. High rent, isn't it?"

"But where can they park, then?"

"Nowhere, that's the point — they're supposed to keep moving on. Here's the clerk. Are we a quorum? Oh, the chairman's missing — finishing breakfast, I expect. No, not a burglar, a baker. Here he is, off we go."

The book on local government, she remembered, said that the chairman would formally declare the meeting open and then ask something about minutes. The Extraordinary Meeting was different. He marched rapidly to the head of the trestle table, rapped once for silence, glared round with dark beady eyes and bristling moustache — a man with no time for nonsense, with a

202

night's baking to do — and announced, "Now then! Sunnink's got to be done about that ruddy common."

It was like a starting-pistol. The councillors' first speeches followed one another rapidly and with real feeling, like a family row continued in public:

"Mr. Chairman! My son and his wife have been waiting years for a place of their own. Why shouldn't *they* take a caravan on the common?"

"Now let's be fair —"

"All right for you! Half a mile away. They use my hedge for a lavatory —"

"Address the chair please."

"All this polio. Flies. It's not right."

"Picnics, we used to have out there. Now it's a blasted holiday camp."

"On our back bricks all day long, asking for water."

"Right, let's give them water. Christ, they're only human. *We've* got it at last, not before time. Give them a standpipe on the common —"

Cries of protest from the floor, sharp raps from the chair.

"I mean it. *And* toilets. Till we get this sorted out."

"Mr. Chairman —"

The chairman nodded to the next speaker.

"I let them use my well, and what thanks do I get? All my best cookers gone."

"Now, now, Mr. Dady. Scrumping's an old tale."

"So're my Rev. Wilkses. Dirty thieving lot."

"Clean enough, give 'em water."

"You can have 'em then. Hand over your orchard — why don't you?"

"You farmers, all you think about's cheap labour."

"Cheap nothing, they're getting the rate."

"Since when?"

"Ninepence a hundredweight potato-picking — like to see the books?"

"Address the chair please."

An elderly woman spoke up bitterly. "My husband worked hard all his life. We retired here for a bit of peace. And what have we got? A car-breaker's yard on our doorstep, bang, bang, bang all day long, and half the night sometimes."

A burst of agreement. As it died down, a very old councillor, with rosy face and silver tonsure, was heard finishing a long anecdote: ". . . lured away with sweets . . . stained with walnut-juice . . . sold abroad . . . Kidnapping, you know, is simply slang for child-stealing. They went about in caravans —"

The chairman intervened. "Not lately, Mr. Mossop, surely?"

"Oh, well, no, not lately. I'm speaking of my grandfather's time."

"About the year of Waterloo," Tony murmured.

The storm was blowing itself out. The meeting seemed to pause, clear its throat and recover its temper before getting down quietly to business: "Constructive action". "A proper site, like the French camp." "Yes, and out of earshot." "Write to the Rural Council first?" A resolution was framed, moved and seconded: their clerk to write to the Rural District Council —

"That's *himself*," Tony whispered.

"Who?"

"The clerk. Young Taplow. In the daytime he's clerk to the Rural Council. So now he'll write himself a letter from the parish. Then he'll write back to himself from the R.D.C . . ."

Soon after that people were beginning to leave, and Rowan slipped out with them. As she went the gipsy policeman was on his feet, with leave from the chair, saying that if a camp were set up he was prepared to leave the Force and offer himself as warden. The gipsies had had a raw deal, no one knew better than . . . the door shut.

She waited a moment, getting used to the twilight. Lights shone across the green, a door opened and shut, radios sounded faintly, a cow called in the distance, trees rustled wildly. Not a mad tea-party, it had all made sense all right. But she felt — not like Alice exactly, but like Alice's sister on the last page: a great deal seemed to have happened in the last few hours, and now she was back to peace and silence, except for these soothing country sounds. It was a relief to be alone and remember.

CHAPTER
TEN

The wind had risen, the black curves of the downs had tossing manes of trees on the skyline. She left her bicycle at the Woodman, a little inn beyond the racing stables, and walked back along the lane past the Grange. A path led eastward up over grassy downs at the rear of the house.

Close to a sunk fence a little grove of stone pines made a desolate sound in the gale. Windows looked out, blank and eerie, across the neglected garden. An iron staircase curved up to a first-floor balcony in front of a glass door. As she went by, Rowan thought she saw a glimmer of light behind the panes. It vanished and did not reappear. A reflection, a car on Diddy-Bone-Snap? But there had been no car. A bicycle, then? Or some ghostly visitant, come back to flit through the deserted rooms at night?

About to hurry on uphill, she noticed something more welcome — a patch of small round objects, snow white, on the overgrown lawn. Too big for daisies. Pebbles, white rose petals? No, mushrooms, she was certain. She jumped across the haha. The iron gate in the fence above was locked and wired, but she climbed over that and crossed the wet grass. They *were* mushrooms. She lifted one carefully. It was white as a pigeon's egg, cold as a snowball, with that warm musty mushroom smell: the smell of autumn, like cobwebs and decaying leaves.

Then she jumped. A sharp rap had sounded on the glass door. It creaked open and someone stood on the balcony; going near, shining her torch, Rowan saw a little old woman who called out something and waved a stick, but the words were blown away. A small dog ran out and began to yelp and caper. The old woman went on peering through the dusk. She had white wispy hair, a black cloak, a light-coloured stick on which she leaned as she called out once more, while she beckoned with her other hand. Rowan went over to the staircase, carrying the mushroom. She said, "I'm sorry. I didn't know anyone was living here already."

"Already!" Three tiny mocking syllables. But she didn't seem annoyed. After all, it was quite easy to explain, "I was picking mushrooms. Would you like them?" The old lady looked down at her, then leaned over the rail and said in a friendly tone, "What I would like, if you'd be so kind, is two or three nice cones."

"*Cones?*"

"Pine cones. You'll find plenty there." Again she waved her stick towards the trees. "For Sneeflocken. He likes to chew them up, it keeps him quiet for hours." The little white woolly dog wriggled and whined. His mistress asked suddenly in a sharper tone, "I suppose those devils have all gone? None of them still lurking about?"

Devils? Rowan stared at her. Was she a bit mad? No: she went on, with a dry look like a thought reader, "Those workmen. They're about the place at all hours nowadays. Rather hard, you know, after fifty years! But I won't be driven out. Flocken and I are camping here in the nursery wing. So — if you *would* be very kind — my slippers are rather thin . . ." They were indeed, and so was their wearer. The cloak fell open, Rowan saw a dry frail little creature in a wrinkled jersey dress. Her arms and legs were like stalks, but her face was oddly pretty for such an old person. The torchlight showed small delicate features, large eyes that might be grey or hazel, an air of gaiety and independence in touching contrast to her fragile looks.

She was right about the cones. Under the stone pines the ground was strewn with them. Groping about, Rowan gathered a handful, dry and flaky like petrified chrysanthemums, and took them back to the balcony. The old lady had retreated out of the wind.

"Come in, my dear child, come in. There, Flocken!"

Camping was the right word, Rowan saw. The room had been cleared for decorating: no curtains, no carpet, an empty grate, not even an electric bulb. The owner was sitting on a folding camp stool; she had lighted a candle and set it beside her in a jam-jar on the floor. Shadows flickered over the walls; the paper, faded and worn, had a design of little green leaves. The room felt very chill, and Rowan exclaimed, "But you haven't any fire!"

"Oh, I'm quite comfortable. I just like to sit out here and see the garden. But in there —" she nodded towards two doors at the back of the room — "*that* was the night nursery."

"Oh, I see . . ." Rowan thought of white-painted beds, fluffy rugs, a huge fire behind a high old-fashioned guard.

"Bathroom next door, and Nanny's little kitchen, all self-contained. I think I shall settle in here, you know. I've had to keep moving round, because of the alterations, and last month I had one of the old guest rooms. Not nearly so convenient." In the candle-light one could see that her eyes were a clear pale brown. She seemed to muse, forgetting Rowan, who turned to go.

"Oh! One moment." She blew out the candle before opening the door. Rowan caught another muttered allusion to "devils" — the workmen seemed very much on her nerves. But she turned and began again quite happily, "We designed this wing ourselves, you see, for our first child. And the magnolia —" she pointed to a tall tree like a laurel beside the balcony, dark leathery leaves flapping in the wind — "that was Mark's tree. All these trees you can see from here — five of them — were planted to celebrate our children."

"What a good idea . . ." And what a dim reply, Rowan thought, blushing in the dark. Still, it *was* a good idea. And she seemed pleased.

"We thought so! A blue cedar, and a copper beech, and a Lombardy poplar. But the lime tree was for me. I love the scent — do you? Lime blossom. My husband chose it so carefully, he said it would grow to be heart-shaped, like a lime leaf, and you see it *has*." But

Rowan could see only wind-blown branches and dead leaves skittering against the panes. She asked, "What was the fifth? The fifth tree," she added, as the old woman didn't answer. "You said — I thought — you had five children . . ."

"Yes," abruptly. "The fifth was a tulip tree. Quite right, yes — that was for Griselda. But it didn't do." Then she added rather formally, "I do hope we'll meet again. But you see how things are just now. I can't have visitors. Later on, I hope . . ." She tottered a little, planted her stick more firmly and opened the door. The dog stopped chewing and tearing the pine cone, and bounced forward.

"No, Flocken, no." Rowan slipped through and heard the key turn behind her. She remembered the mushrooms, but didn't wait to gather them now. She turned up the hood of her windcheater and picked her way over the shaggy grass. Looking back from the pathway, she thought she could see the little figure still watching her, standing close to the panes. The wind roared in the trees, swaying the tall cedar and poplar, raking leaves from lime and copper beech. Rowan thought of the oak sapling just planted at school, their Coronation tree. By contrast, all these looked very old. They might have been planted a hundred years ago.

CHAPTER
ELEVEN

She raced up the hill like a horse that turns for home, and paused for a moment at the top beside a long windbreak of yews, ancient tall trees set close together. The wind hissed between straight trunks silted up with needles. It was dark now, and owls called from covert to covert across the downs as though answering one another.

The path ran away to the north past the old racecourse, where at dawn the horses would come to gallop. She turned away from it, going downhill and then up again to circle the hanger wood, keeping clear of the tossing lower branches. Far away she could see car headlights on the Alchester road. As she watched, one of them seemed to leave the ground and sweep in a great arc through the sky before vanishing — a shooting-star.

She left the hanger and again went down the steep slope towards the faint sound of the river. Her hands touched briars and gorse, her feet stumbled among thick tufts of grass and small thorn bushes, until she found herself on the soft grass of the water meadow. The cattle were gone. Lower still, she was picking her way over marshy ground and rushes. Here were the willows, bright leaves glimmering in the dark. Here was the bridge. She pulled off gumboots and socks, rolled up her jeans, slid down the bank, drew a quick breath and beamed her torch into the black mouth.

It was all right. The willow mats were there still, stacked upright on a brick ledge, a foot deep in water now. She stooped, waded in and drew them out one by one, throwing them up on to the bank.

Taken singly, they were light in the hand. Together they would make a clumsy pile, but it would be best to take them all at once if she could. She lashed them tightly with string into a square pack, twisted several strings into a loop and slowly dragged them up the slope behind her. She had to stop now and then to disentangle the pack from bushes or brambles. When she listened there was no sound but the faint purl of the river behind her, the distant roar of beeches, rustle of blowing grass and once the cry of a moorhen. She toiled on.

Here was the hanger at last. She found the cave and rekindled the fire in the bucket. Smoke and sparks blew about, flames leaped in the wind, but no one was likely to see. She untied the hurdles and ranged them around, to make a screen and to dry them out. Tomorrow, as soon as it was light, she could start to build.

Make me a willow cabin at thy gate . . .

The line came out of nowhere, so suddenly that she was stunned.

212

A wave of grief and loneliness broke over her. After all, she realized, she had been deceiving herself, trying to cling to the past. Her instinct this morning had been right — there was nothing left here now but empty reminders. She was like a child playing house, but far too old for such games. In panic she began to collect her things, wanting only to get away at once, to get back home quickly.

But the moment passed. She thought — I'm tired and hungry, that's all it is. I do want to stay. It's lovely here, and it's mine, nothing to do with him or anyone else. Of course it *is* a sort of game; well, why not? As for being too old, perhaps she had outgrown her parents' home, or outstayed her welcome there. So now was the time to go on and find another.

Sitting down again on the moss, nibbling an apple and a chocolate bar, she felt the sense of desolation gradually slip away. She felt better, and oddly sleepy. She pulled the pile of bracken to the front of the cave, made a nest, wrapped herself in her windcheater and lay down.

Sleep fled at once. All around her, beyond the firelight, darkness was like a blanket; but the night was far from silent. Under the rhythmic crying of the trees she heard stealthy rustlings from all sides, tiny spurts of sound like running mice. Boughs creaked overhead like a ship at sea. Leaves and beechnuts fell, clicking and whispering down from branch to branch. Stars glinted through the shifting foliage. She lay trying to remember the north sky in the star book, the Great Bear, the Pole Star, Little Bear, Cassiopeia, the stars that never set.

213

Houses should be built, she thought, with a starlight roof of glass in each bedroom so that one could always lie and watch them.

She remembered hearing of Merren's disgust when she was offered a "visual aid" for her pupils, a film of the moon sailing over rooftops, to go with a tape recording of a de la Mare poem. A worse shock had followed: the children, on being questioned, blithely admitted that they never noticed the moon except sometimes from a bedroom window. Since then, one of their favourite school outings had been a night picnic held twice a year, in spring and autumn, to look at stars and see the full moon rise from Barrow Hill.

She was growing drowsy when a different sound made her jump and then sit up quickly; a soft padding of feet over the leaves near by. It stopped. Some creature must be out there in the darkness beyond the glow of the fire — watching her, perhaps. She got up and put on more wood, stirring it into a blaze and sitting down close beside it, turning her head this way and that to catch a gleam of yellow eyes in the shadows. She could see nothing. It had sounded quite big — a stray dog, a fox; but neither would attack her. And wolves were all gone . . . how long ago? A century at least.

But she couldn't help recalling with a nasty qualm that not far away there was a country house where rumour said that "lions and tigers" were kept in a private zoo. And one might have escaped? At once she found herself remembering something else; a story she had read about a girl coming home through a wood,

214

seeing a leopard trotting along the road towards her, escaped from a menagerie. The girl climbed a tree and thought herself safe, but of course the leopard could climb too and it came snarling up after her. Just as it came near, she opened a tin of green paint she'd bought in the village, and poured it down into the fearful savage eyes. Rowan couldn't remember what came next, after that terrible scream and fall — some kind of rescue party, she supposed; but no hope of that here. Shaken, she chose a stout stick and pushed it into the fire, sending up a volley of sparks. A blazing brand might come in useful, as there wasn't any green paint handy. She thought of retreating into the cave; but then she would be cornered . . .

Out there a twig cracked sharply. She found herself shivering, put on her jacket again and held her cold hands over the fire, then thrust them into the pockets. Finding some chestnuts she had picked up — oh, long ago, in that beautiful daylight, among the sunny woods and butterflies — she dropped them into the ashes. The whiff of roasting nuts was homely and comforting, evoking London streets after school on a winter day. She set herself to imagine the walk home from Gloucester Road tube station, step by step; along the high slippery pavement under the poplars; up the Old Brompton Road; past Thistle Grove, with its mysterious scent of flowers — ghost flowers, she sometimes thought, from the days when it was a country grove; past the new coffee bars, down into Chelsea . . . then she found that she was thinking instead of the route to her nearest refuge, Merren's cottage. As the crow flew it wasn't far. Which way would be best in the dark, supposing one did want to go there? Not through the trackless wood. Quicker to go back the way she had come, down past the yew fence and the moated grange, then up again to Fitching Down. Or the way she had gone this morning, down to the river, out to the green lane, on by the road? No: that must be miles out of the way. One could take a much shorter way round the edge of the hanger, east and then south-west, plotting a course by the stars, by Pegasus and Andromeda if one could find them, as so often one couldn't. That should bring her out on to Diddy-Bone-Snap, near a stile in the wire fence, where a path led up between the plantations to the cottage.

That would be quickest; not, of course, that she had any idea of following it. Simply reassuring, to know that one *could*. Though really, she told herself, it was too absurd to be sitting here, wide awake, scared by little harmless noises, scampering mice and rabbits. Much better to sleep and forget them; when she opened her eyes again it would be morning. She finished the chestnuts, made up the fire once more and lay down in the bracken.

CHAPTER
TWELVE

Dark pointed firs like Christmas trees stood up around the cottage. A star flashed above the tallest. For a moment Rowan was puzzled by something in the paddock beyond, a curving shape like a tiny Nissen hut in silhouette against the sky. Then she saw that it was an old-fashioned caravan. Somewhere in the darkness a horse stamped and huffled. No lights — the gipsies must be asleep. The cottage was unlighted too, of course, with Merren away; but the key would be in its usual slot above the door.

Odd: it wasn't there. She had to grope her way back to the well and find the "secret" key in a niche between two stones. Suppose that were missing too? No, here it was. Fingers trembling a little, she found the keyhole. She was indoors at last, locking the door again, shutting out the night. The smell of the cottage enfolded her, warm and friendly as a cat's fur. She took deep breaths of it — paraffin, wood fires, fir cones, apples, celery, mice — before putting out her hand to the table. There were matches to hand as usual; she struck one, lit a candle in a blue-and-white china holder and carried it into the sitting-room.

The gate-legged table was laid with three places: blue Spode cups and saucers, knives and forks, the wooden biscuit barrel garlanded with gold bees — carved long ago by one of those men in the camp. She wondered what meal this was meant for and who the other guests would be. But she knew Merren wouldn't mind her coming. She drew the curtains, put a match to the fire — that was laid ready too — and sat happily watching it. After the cave in the windy hanger, the scrambling cross-country walk in the dark, the cottage felt like a little fortress.

Presently she picked up the candle and began to prowl about, drawn first as usual to the school groups on the wall. There was Merren's first class at a village school somewhere, dated 1930; rows of rather scared-looking urchins with crew-cut heads, heavy jerseys, lumpy flannel jackets, thick boots or thin "plimsolls"; and beside it, Ralph and his friends at a prep school in 1939; grey-flannelled too, and by his own account no better fed, but less careworn. Merren said that at both schools the children were over-exercised and under-nourished; now, she thought, the tendency was the other way round. Anyway, the third picture was quite different — a large coloured photograph of the Fitching children laughing in the snow, in their enhanting modern chain-store clothes, thin soft jerseys, tartan trews, bright ski-jackets, with their donkey, goats and rabbits.

Over the sofa she found something new: a framed map of the district. A presentation map, perhaps — Merren's cottage stood in the middle, beautifully drawn, with a beehive on one side and a henhouse on the other. Names were in Indian ink, in italic writing; symbols for meadow and marsh, conifers and deciduous woods, roads, rivers and railways, Roman and Ancient British remains, were all in coloured inks. It was signed at the bottom by half a dozen names. She knelt on the sofa searching for one place after another from her journey of today. (Or yesterday? the little travelling-clock was gone, she had no idea if it might be midnight yet.) The lane with the cache tree, she saw, was called Linkhorn Lane; the farm, Chalk Farm; the wood, Cut and Lie Wood. A little race-horse depicted the stables. She found the Grange, the common with a gipsy caravan, Fitching and Alderton, Holt with its tiny chapel lost in the fields. And there in the north-west corner was the house she had been thinking of — Tatsworth, shown with a little yellowy cat's head, leopard or puma, behind bars . . .

She moved along to find the vole river, the cattle bridge, the hanger wood. Then she cried out, "Oh!" and knelt upright, holding the candle nearer. It didn't seem possible, but it was true: the hanger wood was named Hermitage.

So perhaps the cave was really ancient, a refuge for some anchorite or some fugitive of long ago? If only Merren were here to tell her! It was too exasperating to make such a discovery, with no way of following it up.

But, if the name were an old one, there must be a legend; perhaps she could find that in a guide-book or a county history. She crossed the room to search

Merren's bookcase. No — nothing. Any books of that kind were probably down at the school.

Scanning the lowest shelf, she lighted on a title never seen before, yet somehow familiar. *The Proud Gunner*. Hadn't Lesley done a jacket for that — her first, too? She prised out the slim volume. Yes: "drawings by Lesley Fraser". Black and white scraperboard jacket, a great dark sea-cave, white furry seal cub, white pebbles, white-capped waves, touched as with luminous paint; an eerie atmosphere, like moonlight, or a photographic negative.

She read on the title page:

It shall come to pass on a summer day
When the sun lies hot on every stone
That I will take my little young son
And teach him for to swim the foam.

And you shall marry a proud gunner,
And a proud gunner I'm sure he'll be.
And the very first shot that e'er he shoots
He'll shoot both my young son and me.

There was a frontispiece, a seal and its cub, beside the sea. Flicking over the pages to look for other drawings, she came on a loose paper like a bookmark. A cutting from a newspaper; something about elephant seals. She began to read, tried to stop and found that she couldn't. "*They battered them over the head with long poles so that their eyes were burst and knocked out, and stuck knives into them — I have seen a whole* side ripped open and guts hanging out — chopped off the ends of the tail flippers . . . iron bars rammed into their throats . . . so that they got down to the beach with broken jaws and splintered teeth."

But that must have been in the bad old days, it couldn't be happening now: could it? She looked at the cutting again, and it seemed that she was mistaken . . . She replaced the book on the shelf. Presently she lay down on the sofa, looking into the fire, trying to think of ordinary heartening things. The silence seemed menacing.

She had slept uneasily for a long time when a nightmare began. Everything at first was black and white. She was in the Hermitage, and around her were wolves with snapping teeth. Then there was black water, and white pebbles like glow-worms. She tried to pick one up, and all was changed. Now she was in school — that night last term — and there was a nun, the spectre in *Villette*, running past, going to climb up a rope in the gym. But that was fearfully dangerous: Rowan tried to run after her, tried to shout a warning. She couldn't catch up, no sound would come, and the struggle woke her.

The fire was nearly out, the candle low in its socket, but she wasn't in the dark. Thank goodness. She lay still, telling herself that everything was all right; but her hands felt clammy and the feeling of dread persisted. That man Tony had told them about — he was dead by the time they cut him down. As for the seal piece . . . she shuddered, the candle guttered. She got up to look for a new one before it could go out. But something made her turn her head quickly towards the window. She listened. A footstep? Not a dog or a fox this time, either . . . but of course it couldn't have been a person. Who would be coming here in the middle of the night? She really must not start *listening* again: that was what had gone wrong, up in the hanger. She leaned across the rug to put more logs on the hot ashes, and began to blow at them gently with the bellows. Then she heard the step again.

She hadn't been mistaken. Quiet measured steps, and a shadow on the curtain. Someone was walking round the cottage. A beam of torchlight travelled over the ceiling. She thought she heard someone trying the door; then back the footsteps came, and paused outside the window.

Instinctively she had blown out the candle and crouched down out of sight. There was a loud knocking on the window, and a man's voice called, "Who's in there?" Then, when she was expecting to die of fright, he called again — "Come on, who is it? Open up — *police!*"

She sprang up. The relief was so great, for a moment she felt almost too weak to walk to the door. She stumbled into the kitchen and tripped over her gumboots. There was more knocking, at the door now, and again the word, "Police!" She called hoarsely, "Just a minute . . ." found her torch and switched it on before turning the key.

The door swung open. The man on the step wasn't in uniform, as she had expected, but in an ordinary

222

raincoat. He turned a powerful torch on her face, dazzling her. She stepped back, holding the door for him to come in. At that he lowered the torch and seemed to look a little less grim. He said, "Now, miss. How do you know I'm really a policeman? Supposing I was having you on — eh?"

She looked at him blankly. How *did* she know? The thought of a hoax had never crossed her mind — odd, considering the many alarms that *had* crossed it that night.

"You should've asked to see my warrant card. Here you are," and he produced something like a large season ticket in a transparent holder. She saw a crest or coat of arms at the top, and underneath, "This is to certify that Roy Lamb holds the rank of Detective Sergeant . . . This is his warrant and authority . . . signed, Chief Constable . . . signature of holder, Roy Lamb." As he took it back and stepped in, he explained in quite a friendly tone, "Miss McKay told us she'd be away tonight. Then I saw your light, so I thought I'd have a look."

"But — could you really see one candle? All the way from Fitching?" The words reminded her of something. *How far that little candle throws his beams . . .*

"So shines a good deed in a naughty world," the officer finished thoughtfully, and grinned at her look of surprise. He picked up the matches and lit the lamp. He had a mass of grey curly hair, but his face looked young. He said, "No, I was down on the road, driving past. Told her I'd keep an eye on the place."

She felt compelled to explain, "She didn't know I was coming, I just dropped in. Look, shall I make a cup of tea? I was just going to, I had a nightmare, then I heard you out there and I got an awful fright." Reaction was making her chatter. She had an idea that policemen didn't accept refreshment while on duty — or was that only *drink*? However, he seemed to have no objection, and began to light the primus for her. Watching the blue flames, she asked on impulse, "Did you come because of those threats?"

"Ah. Now, what threats were you thinking of?"

"I don't really know. Only Tony Markwick said — something about anonymous letters?"

"Who said?"

She found Tony's card in her pocket and handed it over. He peered at it, one eye on the stove, and laughed.

"I see. A vulture of the Press." He pumped the stove into a steady roar, put on the little tea kettle, looked at her again and asked, "You know about the paddock, do you? And the Fallas?"

"Only what Tony said — she's given them a bit of land to live on, because of the children."

"H'm. Yes. Lease might have been better. Too late now, though."

She could not follow this. Seeing her look mystified, he added, "So now she's stuck with them, you see. Right on her doorstep. She gave it to them, deed and all — any trouble, she's in it too. Not that *they'd* make any . . ."

"Trouble?" Tony Markwick had said "trouble" too. But Sergeant Lamb seemed to have said all he meant to, on that topic. He asked one more brief question — ". . . she take her cat with her?"

"Yes."

He nodded, and they watched the kettle get up steam. She was making up her mind to ask about something else. In the sitting-room, with lamp and teacups, the fire crackling cheerfully, he leaned back in a chair, stirring his tea; but before she could begin, he asked, "You'll be staying till tomorrow? Back tomorrow night, she said."

She hesitated. "Well — I'll come back, I expect . . ." and wished she had just said, "Yes." Questions about her own plans might lead to the Hermitage.

He took a sip, put down his cup and said, "Glad to find you here. Left your bike at the Woodman, didn't you?"

"Oh! Oh, yes — but how — ?"

"Landlord reported, when you weren't back by midnight."

It wasn't going to be easy, one saw, to keep a secret in the country. By way of a red herring, she said quickly, "You know that road — Linkhorn Lane? — Along past the Woodman, half a mile or so, there's a tree burnt out. Was that lightning, do you know?"

"Past Chalk Farm?"

She glanced up at the map. "Yes, that's it . . ."

"I know the tree you mean. No, not lightning. Boys with home-made gunpowder, last year. Tree went up like a torch, and smouldered for days, right to a cinder."

"Oh . . ." She thought of the manhole last night. "They do that sort of thing in Chelsea too."

"I dare say. And if you look at old police reports, hundred years ago, you find they were doing it then. Boys don't change much — young monkeys."

"Supposing —" She began again, and stopped.

"Yes?"

"Oh, I just thought — suppose there'd been something hidden inside? It would all have got burnt, wouldn't it? Or — might they have got it out?"

"Something hidden?"

"Oh, you know — a cache. Papers and stuff?"

"Go on," he encouraged. "Papers and what stuff?"

Sitting there in the lamplight, he looked alert and friendly, easy to talk to. So she went on, and told him about the cache. No point in secrecy now that it was burnt.

He seemed quite surprisingly interested. "A hoard in a hollow tree? I see. H'm! And what was your cousin's name?" He actually took out a notebook and wrote that down, like a stage policeman. She had a sudden gleam of hope; perhaps, after all, something had been found and handed in? She was going to ask, when he surprised her again: "Ralph Oliver — and he used to live in Ireland, didn't he?"

How could he know that? She hadn't said anything about Ireland. She nodded, expecting more. But he only said mysteriously, "If I hear anything, I'll let you know." The notebook was put away. She gave him a discontented look, and he smiled, passing his cup for more tea. As she filled it he asked, "And you'll be down here till — when?"

"Oh, Monday morning, I expect. Early, though."

"School on Monday?"

"School on Tuesday. Prep on Monday — I suppose." Those essays! Yes, she would have to get back on Monday. Even so, she might have to sit up all night to finish them. The thought brought on a tremendous yawn, and he stood up.

"That's right, you get some sleep. Tell Miss McKay we'll be around tomorrow night — not that she worries. Up here on her own, though . . ." He was putting on his coat.

A thought struck her, and she asked sleepily, "Do you keep an eye on the Grange too?"

"On where?"

"Fitching Grange. That old lady — she's on her own too, isn't she?"

He looked round. "What was that again?"

His voice sounded quite odd. She repeated, "The Grange . . ."

"And? What old lady?"

Really astonished now, she stammered, "You know. That lives there, that owns it. I was talking to her."

He still eyed her, his face expressionless. She added, "At the back, you know, in that nursery flat. I got her some cones for her dog."

He said slowly and heavily, "Oh dear, oh dear, oh dear." He stood still, shaking his head, not looking at her. "Not in there again, is she!" He sounded taken aback, upset, and yet somehow — amused, could it be? But there must be some mistake. She explained, "I meant — Fitching Grange, the house in the trees, that they're making into flats."

He was still shaking his head, clicking his tongue, registering dismay; but he wasn't being mysterious, as he had been about Ralph. He exclaimed quietly, as though half to himself, "Oh, why can't they look after her! Prison this time, it'll have to be. How she gets in there, that's the mystery — place swarming with workmen all day long."

"I don't see — what do you mean, prison? It's her house, isn't it?" *Could* they be talking about the same place? "She's got her key, of course!"

"Ho, got a key this time, has she!" He was chuckling openly.

Rowan heard her own voice quavering as she said, "You . . . do you mean . . . it was all made up? About her children, and — the garden, and everything? You mean, she's *mad*?"

He stopped laughing then. "Mad? Mrs. Covey? Not she. Obstinate, though. And clever."

Rowan said miserably, "I don't understand. She said she'd lived there for years, she said it was hers."

"Oh yes, that's true enough. It was hers. Till her husband died, and left all sorts of debts, and a mortgage she'd never heard of. So then it was all sold up, you see — only she won't have it, poor soul. Her married daughter found her a nice room somewhere, a hotel in London I believe — but no, she will insist the Grange is her home and she's going to live there. The first time, she barricaded herself in a bedroom, took them days to get her out, and she was back before they could turn round. They had to take her to court in the end. Twice she's been up now, or is it three times?"

"But — *court*? Whatever for?"

"County court. It's trespass, you see, but they tried to explain — old Judge Timperley, he didn't like it a bit. He keeps saying she's no idea what a prison cell would be like, trying to make her promise she won't get in again. But she told him she'd made up her mind to go on living there, and she wouldn't mind going to prison, and she'll do it again directly they let her out. Last time he said he'd give her one more chance."

Rowan cried, "Oh, don't tell anyone! Need you? She's not doing any harm!"

"Oh, they'll find out soon enough — probably know by now. Security patrol, you know." He turned back again to ask, "Notice if she's got a candle?"

"Oh yes. Yes, she has. In a jam-jar."

"There you are, you see. She could get burnt to death." Rowan did see. But — prison? That fragile dignified little person? She said haltingly, "I wish she could have just one more day there. She — I think, if they let her do that, she might go away afterwards. Perhaps she's just — you know — sort of making a last protest." She could not explain why she thought this; but he said slowly:

"I know. It's hard on her. But don't you worry too much. It's something, you know, to have them all in a spin — I dare say she's enjoying herself, in her own way."

He was gone; and he hadn't promised anything. She stood in the doorway looking out at the dark sky and faint stars. The wind had dropped, the air was icy, mist drifted in. The owls were still calling in the woods. Perhaps she ought to go down at once, to warn Mrs. Covey? But she would be asleep: wouldn't she? And it was so dark, the darkest hour before the dawn.

CHAPTER
THIRTEEN

She was roused by a soft persistent tapping sound, like a child at the window. Before she opened her eyes, she thought of the gipsy children. Then she heard flutterings, tiny lisping notes, a shrill clear whistle, and realized what it was. Merren's tomtits and nuthatch were taking peanuts from the gutter, where she left food for them out of Badger's reach.

She lay back, stretching comfortably — she was warmly wrapped in the eiderdown from Merren's bed, but could hardly recall fetching it. She had felt so drowsy after her long day, after Sergeant Lamb's departure, and all that talk.

Then she remembered. Mrs. Covey! She had meant to go down at daybreak. Now it was broad daylight, anything might be happening, and she hadn't warned her. She rushed into windcheater and boots, not stopping to wash or brush her hair; tousled as she was, that would have to wait. She *must* scribble a note for Merren, in case she got back first and thought the place had been burgled. That didn't take long. Slinging on her rucksack, she was half out of the door when she looked back and was smitten with guilt: she spent three

231

frantic minutes rinsing cups and sketchily tidying the sitting-room, then left it all and fled.

But there was no answer to her knock. Peering through the glass door, she called, "Mrs. Covey, Mrs. Covey . . ." Silence. The room was empty. Had they taken her away already? Her things were still in there on the floor; a zipped hold-all, the camp stool, the matchbox. Not the candle — that was gone. So she was probably still asleep in the "night nursery". Again she knocked and called. The only sound was from a fly fussing inside the glass. She left the balcony and walked all round the house, over long wet grass, through shrubberies, past uncurtained windows, back to where she had started; no one was about. The mushrooms, already past their brief youth, were flat now and going brown at the edges.

What next? Well, she could come back later. And leave a note for now. No paper, though; and she had left her pencil at the cottage. She fell back on childhood resources, a magnolia leaf, a sharp thorn from one of the rosebeds; cutting this off carefully with her penknife, because of Grandmother's warning: old rose thorns give you blood poisoning. She printed in capitals, pale green on dark green, THEY KNOW YOU ARE HERE, and slid the leaf under the balcony door.

There seemed nothing more she could do. But suddenly she changed her mind, bent down and drew the leaf out again, groping for it with the knife blade. After all, what was the use of warning her? Better than anyone else, she knew what would happen. Let her stay in peace as long as she could, with all her thoughts of the past. She crumpled the leaf in her hand and ran away across the garden.

From the pathway she could see across to that little new house up by the beech spinney; empty, with no ghosts yet and no history, waiting for its future to start.

She was jerked from this reverie by cries and whinnyings in the distance, down by the crossroads. A dozen children and ponies were gathered on the grass at the roadside — a pony club meet? She couldn't help going down to see. As she drew near, a van like a horse-box appeared from Linkhorn Lane; it drew up on the grass, a man jumped out and opened the back. She saw that he was a travelling smith. The old smithy in the village had long been shut, nettles and docks grew round its doors that were still hung with rusty horseshoes. This young smith had all his gear in the van, and the children queued up to have the ponies shod, watching him while he worked just as country children had always gathered to watch what was going on in the smithy. Rowan stood near, watching too, and then looking in a bemused way at the waiting ponies.

One was pale grey with dark mane and tail; it turned on her the mild kind eye she remembered, so that she had to whisper, "Foxglove, Foxglove", and put a hand to its neck. Of course it wasn't Foxglove; yet she felt so strange — almost light-headed really; lack of sleep, perhaps — she wouldn't have been surprised at anything. Still in that half dazed, half-dreaming way, she thought — What in the world am I doing, over here, living in London, still at school, wasting my life —

when all the time I could be there in Ireland with the horses?

At the same time, like someone asleep who knows he is dreaming, she told herself this was only a mood; evoked by the ponies, their long soft coats, their wilful engaging faces, the familiar smells of sweat and grass and leather. Evoked too by simple envy of their owners, who lived here in the country — as she meant to do. And she had started already, yesterday; no need to be envious of anyone. She couldn't live at Nine Wells — no use bringing that up again. Let the Trim boys have it. She had the Hermitage to build, and a whole day to get it done.

Another rider was coming along the lane. It looked like that boy, what was his name? Bobby? — on a different, quieter mount. She didn't want him to see her again. She turned and walked back into the mist, on towards the hidden sunlight in the east. This queer mood would soon go when she had dipped her face in the river and brewed a can of hot tea.

It went before that. As she stood on the bank, shaking drops of water from her hair, she heard a sound she knew well; the gentle *cloop* of a water vole diving. She looked downstream and saw it swimming, bubbles of water streaming. The sun broke through. The water vole swam down a flare-path of white light and disappeared. The last vole of summer, she thought. That was a lovely moment.

She found the box trap on the grass where she had dropped it yesterday, and hid it in the pigeon-hole; spared a thought for the two boys moping in

234

quarantine, hoped the card had arrived; and ran up the slope to the Hermit-age.

She spent a happy morning fitting the willow hurdles among the great roots inside and out of the cave; thatching with moss and bracken, securing the thatch with ropes of old-man's-beard. Then she worked for an hour collecting firewood, a dreamily obsessive search for more and more twigs, logs, withered branches, until she was too hungry to go on. She had left potatoes baking in the ashes; now she sat down to scoop the white delicious fluff out of the thick black skins, to toast sausages, then to lie on the moss drinking coffee and thinking over all the events of yesterday.

Midges hovered in shafts of misty sunlight. The October wood was brilliant emerald, touched with all the colours of the year; crocus-yellow fungus, primrose bracken, wildrose spindle fruits, beech leaves with the tender gold of May, toadstools coloured grey and scarlet like fires in January mist. A different world from the one she had shivered in last night. But tonight she might come back, and this time there should be no cowardly fancies.

In her note to Merren she had said she would call in at the cottage — better start soon, so that she could be here again before dark.

She was ready to go when she suddenly noticed tracks leading up from the water-meadows, more tracks criss-crossing in and out of the wood: all leading directly to the cave. Could she have made all those? Anyone coming here had only to follow them to find the place. She set about covering them, combing the pale grass of the hill with branches, scattering leaves in the wood. She seemed to have been at it only a few minutes, but all at once the sun was in the west, the hanger full of shadows.

And what about Mrs. Covey?

All was quiet as she came near the Grange. The dark pines, the tawny copper beech, pale lime and spiky silvery cedar seemed motionless, brooding in the twilight. Only the poplar shivered a little.

No sign of Mrs. Covey; no answer to her calls. But the things were gone from the floor. Nothing was left but a few flakes of pine cone. Something must have happened. The door was still locked, the glass intact: at least they hadn't smashed their way in to get her. Perhaps after all she had saved them the trouble, given in at last — she might have packed up and left before anyone came, and gone away back to London, to that hotel room arranged by her daughter.

Oh, but it was all wrong; it should never have happened . . . *the shuddering of that dreadful day, When friend and fire and home are lost, And even children fall away* . . .

Rowan thought — I was right last night about a ghost. She'll haunt this house. And I hope I never hear what's happened today.

CHAPTER
FOURTEEN

Half-way up Diddy-Bone-Snap she met the caravan from the paddock; a brown wooden van with a horseshoe canopy set with coloured panels. The Fallas were all there in a bunch behind the skewbald horse: going to the fair at Alchester? Dark and serious-looking, they went by without a glance, Father holding the reins, Mother in a bright head-scarf and gold earrings, the boy and girl in jeans and sweaters like any other children. Soon perhaps they would be wearing the grammar school blazer. She thought of them climbing this hill in the evening, going home to their caravan to eat rabbit stew cooked in a black pot over the open fire; doing their prep, algebra and French and science, by firelight and lantern light. They would have the best of both worlds: or — not?

Long before she reached the cottage she saw the lights. How different, again, from last night's arrival. Two cars were parked under the fir trees, the place was crammed with people, six of them round the lamplit table: Merren, Lesley, a follower of hers named Guy, who taught in an art school, and three of his students, tough bearded young men, and the two cats, Badger and Tray. Guy, she had heard, was a sculptor. Seeing him for the first time, she thought this an amazing coincidence: his head was so like an art-room sculpture photograph. A Roman head, beaky, formidable, with large eyes, dark blue, and just the right expression of faint amusement. He must know about the likeness, she decided — it was underlined by the way he wore his hair; short and flat, cut in a straight fringe. And he was silent: one couldn't imagine the Lansdowne Marbles gossiping. The rest talked at the tops of their voices, pleased at the idea of a night siege.

A siege, Rowan gathered, was really in prospect. One of the famous anonymous letters was on show, being passed from hand to hand; containing, not threats, but a mysterious warning. The writer had uncovered a plot: a gang was coming up tonight from Alchester, after the fair, to set fire to the gipsy caravan, and perhaps the cottage as well; to pay her out for befriending the gipsies. The letter was neatly printed in black ink on hairy lined paper and signed in classic form, "Well-Wisher". The spelling was erratic, the word warn being spelt "worn", and friend, "fernd".

Merren laughed at the whole thing, carving an enormous ham and doling out rice pudding from a haybox, with cream and blackberry jam. She admitted that she'd had several letters like that. So had the Fallas; that was why they had decided, belatedly, to go away for a night or two, now that she had company. They didn't want the children mixed up in any trouble. Had she told the police? No need: Well-Wisher had showered letters on them too.

238

For the past three days the traditional autumn fair and livestock sale had been going on at Alchester, ending tonight. The rumours had travelled far and wide; Lesley, hearing of them through an old friend, a land girl married and living at Beaumarsh, had passed them on to Guy, who promptly collected a bodyguard. The students would stay here tomorrow, while Guy and Lesley went on for the day to Gray Gavine, the Dorset house where they had met in the summer while Guy was looking after the art collection. Tabby was at Clare Hall, visiting her grandmother; they would pick her up on Sunday evening.

Supper ended with an alert — a crowd of youths had been sighted, coming up the track from Fitching, bicycle lights flashing and bells ringing. More well-wishers, they proved; ex-pupils of Merren's, eager for the fray. They went on their way to the fair, promising to come back later. Merren sighed.

The two cars, an estate van and a veteran open tourer, were driven close to the garden fence and the headlights turned on while the kitchen copper and zinc bath were filled from the well. Weapons of all kinds were produced. Guy confiscated a shotgun. All had brought sleeping-bags, but no one expected to sleep.

Indoors, Merren closed the old wooden storm-shutters, unused since the wartime blackout ended nine years before. Painted over, the folding panels were stuck together and had to be prised apart with knives. In the kitchen they found another visitor hovering, one of the Fitching boys who had turned back: "Guess I just thought I'd kinda hang around," he said, chewing

239

gum. He was about fourteen, young for his age and on the weedy side, with hair, eyes and skin all of the same fawnish sallow colour, like string. The whole clan had answered to names like Chuck, Rick and Clark; this one was suitably called Hank.

Though drab, he was polite and amiable, entertaining them with tales of gang warfare in Alchester. Then he began to make lurid prophecies about tonight. Merren, cutting vast loaves into sandwiches — "Five barley loaves", she said, unpacking her basket — remained unmoved. This was just a picnic, she lightly conveyed, for a few young friends: what could be nicer? Discouraged, the boy lapsed into silence, devouring crusts as though famished. She fed him with sandwiches.

It occurred to Rowan then that her manner had changed; it was no longer casual and amused but almost lecturing, her tone firm and pointed. The police, she said, had decided to ignore the whole affair — this time. But any repetition, any more of these letters, trying to frighten people, would be a different matter. The whole business would be sifted, handwriting experts would be brought in and the culprit traced at once.

"Oh, them!" Hank laughed. "As if anyone used their proper writing on a job like this! Disguised, it would be, and no dabs either."

"Disguised or not, it would make no difference. They can tell who wrote something — it *is* like fingerprints."

Before he or Rowan could answer, Lesley flew in for a torch: Tray had run off in the dark and couldn't be

240

found. Rowan went after her. Guy and Lesley roamed away through the pine wood, calling and flashing.

She stood still for a moment; pitch dark at first, her surroundings gradually emerged in faint starlight. A wind blew in from the sea, swishing the broom hedge. The three students were prone under their car, tinkering away; an electric lantern shone dimly. She took the path down towards the plantations, crying, "Puss, puss." The high wire fence had a stile now. Climbing on to it, looking out towards the lights of Alchester, she thought she could make out a brighter glow than usual on this side, where the fairground was. It would be in full swing by now. Why shouldn't they all go? She pictured the roar and brilliance, the rush of the switchback railway and the swing of swingboats . . . But, of course, the whole point was to stay here and repel attack. Hank said there might be fifty coming, with bicycle chains and coshes. She thought of Sergeant Lamb's assurances, and hoped that that police decision of which Merren had spoken, "ignoring the whole thing", didn't apply tonight. Really, Merren seemed over-confident. Just a silly joke, she said: but how could she be so sure? Tony Markwick had taken it seriously; so had Sergeant Lamb. And Guy: at least, he'd agreed with Lesley that they ought to bring reinforcements.

She had forgotten about Tray; but now a tiny sound reminded her. It came from close by, high up in a thicket of larches. She turned her head. There it was again. Beaming the torch upward, she saw the cat clinging to the very tip of a tree, stiff with terror. She called; he did not move, but he gave a louder wail.

241

Jumping down from the stile, she let the torch slip from her hand. While she was groping for it someone brushed past her. When she got to the tree, Hank was already swarming up. A few minutes later he dropped to the ground with Tray fastened like a burr to his jersey. Hank was covered with larch needles; with scratches too, no doubt. Dislodging the cat, she explained, "It's not his fault. He thinks there's a window waiting at the top of every tree." Hank muttered something, then turned away and lugged a bicycle from under a bush, swung on to the saddle and went away down the path towards the road. The little red light vanished.

Lesley had had a bad half-hour, faced with the thought of telling Tabby that her cat was lost. Her gratitude, when Rowan appeared, soon led to an invitation: wouldn't she like to come with them tomorrow and see Gray Gavine? Rowan had meant to go to the cave; but, when Guy exerted himself to second this, she found herself quickly accepting and then fading away, like Hank, before they could thank her again.

In the kitchen she found Merren standing by her old range. Badger sat at the far end of the hob, away from the fire, gazing at a large coffee percolator on one of the hot rings. Told of Hank's gallantry, Merren nodded.

"He was a nice little boy. Harry, he was called, before that Hank nonsense." She added, "I wish I had him now. He wasn't ready for a big tough school."

"He's at the grammar school?"

"He's at — a very good school," she said; and then, "Oh, that wretched eleven-plus", and she did something fierce to a damper.

"He didn't pass?"

"Harry? Not a chance. His father and mother were very disappointed, though." She sounded tired and sad. She said slowly, " 'Mankind's greatest problem is intellectual inequality.' Who said that? Buchan, wasn't it?"

Outside, someone began to strum at a guitar. Rowan waited. It was like a crisis in a film: revelation was coming.

The twanging quickened. Presently she went on:

"No, he didn't pass. Hopeless at arithmetic. English? Well, he had imagination. And he wrote neatly. I'd know his handwriting anywhere — I taught him to read and write. In the end. But he couldn't spell. The same mistakes time after time — poor child." The pot gave a lurch, coffee began to swirl and leap inside the glass. They were silent, watching it.

CHAPTER
FIFTEEN

High wrought-iron gates stood between a lane and a grass-grown drive half a mile from the house at Gray Gavine. They were locked, the drive disused, but a little swing gate at the side gave entry to a footpath through the woods.

Guy dropped them here because Lesley wanted Rowan to see the wood-walk first. He drove on to the house, where he had a job waiting: a repair to some wood carving, which he hadn't had time to finish in the summer.

The gates were decorated in a pattern of fronds and spirals around the Gray crest, a badger head — "gray", Lesley thought, was an old heraldic name for the badger, which had lived here unmolested even in the worst days of badger-baiting and unenlightened game-keeping.

They followed the path through buff-coloured oak woods, still splashed here and there with vivid green, and came to a dark tunnel of firs and pine trees, opening into a blaze of light: an aisle of wych elms burning in pale sunlit yellow. It was like going from a shadowy cloister into a lighted cathedral.

244

From another swing-gate the path led down among drifts of leaves, hiding the long grass under the elms, into a wild garden. Ancient fruit trees, bent and mossy, were covered with crimson apples and little hard pears like wilding fruit. In spring, Lesley said, the old trees had the finest blossom she had ever seen, great clusters of snow and coral and silver cherry. Birds built in every tree, in the laurel thickets and briar hedges.

The garden this month was at its wildest. The grass under the trees, cut in June, was a tangle of withering bents, hogweed, yarrow, ground elder, with glimpses of scarlet cuckoopint berries. By January all that would have died down, and the young green grass would be filled with snowdrops, then daffodils, grape hyacinths, sky-blue scillas. Violets from garden frames had been planted there in beds among the fruit trees. A grove of hazels would be carpeted with primroses, cuckoopints and cowslips. Later there were tulips, bluebells and forget-me-nots in the long grass, mixed up with white cow-parsley and green twayblade.

Lesley, coming here first in March, had fallen in love with the pré, as it had always been called. The place was a special favourite too with old Mrs. Gray, who still lived here in her own part of the house and ran the gardens herself, although nowadays she spent the winter abroad. The estate had passed to her son, a successful businessman; but he had never cared much for country life, and lived most of the year in London.

The grounds beyond the wood were enclosed by low iron fences wire-meshed against rabbits. The pré was sheltered on three sides by deep laurel hedges with a

245

carved wooden door at either end. Exploring by herself, while Lesley went off to a potting-shed, Rowan found a water-garden full of tinkling streams and pools, giant leaves, scented shrubs, a little Japanese-looking summerhouse: she had seen that before, in that painting in the garret. The other door led into a walled flower garden with heliotrope and Michaelmas daisies, and a distant view of the grey stone house through garlands of wistaria. The air was filled with sweet dry scents, verbena, geranium and lavender.

She turned back to the wild garden, that smelled of grass and withering elm leaves, with a yeasty tang of rotting fruit; butterflies flew up from a heap of brown apples. She found Lesley and Tray in a shed hidden inside the laurels; called "Trussler's shed" after an old gardener who had been at Gray Gavine for fifty years. He had started there as one of a score of men; now most of the gardens and orchards were leased to a nursery firm, and only one or two part-timers still worked in the grounds close to the house. That was how Lesley, staying here for the summer with Tabby, had come to be taken on when she grew bored with gate-keeping.

Trussler's shed was kept in good order, with tools hanging on nails, and neat shelves to hold tins, labels, balls of string and other oddments. There was a potting-bench with mounds of sieved soil, leaf mould and sand; stacks of seedboxes and tiers of pots; a tub and scrubbing-brush, a box of broken crocks, a birch broom, bunches of sweet-smelling raffia, a water pipe and tap newly swathed in sacking against the first frosts. Also there were homelike touches, a little stove, kettle and teapot, tobacco tin, spare boots and raincoat, a box seat. It was like the cave, Rowan thought; a second home. In London parks and gardens, places like this were hidden out of sight. One had to search and trespass quietly to find them, but they were always more interesting than hothouses and flowerbeds.

Then she began to wonder: could I do this sort of thing? Tony Markwick had said the way to live in the country would be to have a job there. Gardening was a practical idea. One could go to college and be trained — her parents would approve. She began to pay attention.

Lesley had unpacked a parcel of bulbs and was dusting them with mouse repellent and sorting them ready for planting: snowdrops to go near a bed of ivy, yellow aconites to flower with celandines under the hazels, silvery winter crocuses to spread over the grass; but first the basket of primroses: old double whites and sulphurs, they were going under a clump of sallow willows . . .

They planted away for an hour, and it seemed idyllic. Mistletoe like green wishbones hung from an apple bough. A robin sang; red admirals flitted and feasted. Tray dozed in the basket. But the second hour brought doubts. Could one spend whole days like that? Already she was aching, hot and thirsty, secretly impatient for a change of occupation. Breakfast, at a hotel in the New Forest, seemed a long time ago. Lesley kept saying, "Just a few more", and "I'll just put these in" — clearly it was like gathering fuel in the Hermitage wood: if you were really enjoying it you found it hard to stop. But at last she decided to leave the final batch for later.

They went through the walled garden, across a terrace and a paved stableyard, up into the flat she and Tabby had in the summer: two rooms in a turret, part of a structure far older than the Queen Anne house. A wide deep-set window with small diamond panes looked out on to a greensward shaded by oak trees. The walls were of stone, hung with grey tapestry; but also there were thick carpets, electric lighting, a heater and small enamelled stove. Lesley made coffee and produced sandwiches and cake.

Guy appeared presently, and with him two other young men, one bringing a dish of pears and grapes. Lesley already knew these handsome young Italians; trained in hotel work, they now looked after the house, and the three visitors ate their lunch while Angelo amused them with local gossip. Dark and lively, he seemed to find English rural life irresistibly funny. But the other — Ettray, his name sounded like — seemed to Rowan more attractive altogether: quiet, fair and romantic-looking, with a soft voice enhanced by his charming accent. At the first pause in Angelo's recital, he asked after Tabby and made some polite remark regretting that she hadn't come today.

Angelo began to describe a whist drive they had been to in the village; where, for some technical reason, never fathomed, they had found they must represent women. Tray took advantage of this nonsense to filch a piece of cake. Ettray was leaning back in the window seat, sunlight weaving in his hair, humming to himself.

248

And suddenly Rowan knew who it was he reminded her of: that actor to whom she'd lost her heart at Tabby's age, the one who rode Grandfather's Decima in the Battle of Agincourt. She still had his picture somewhere. And — of course! — Tray was named after *this* fascinator. Like Lesley, she found herself thinking rather grimly, Poor little toad.

She wandered about the pré in the mellow sunlight, searching for sweet apples to feed a bunch of horses that came to lean over the hedge from the field. Lesley was finishing the bulbs. Soon they would have to leave, to fetch Tabby, drive back to Fitching with Rowan, then on to London. The three students were staying on at the cottage tonight as a precaution, though nothing had happened last night. Rowan meant to stay too, get up at dawn, fetch her bicycle from the Woodman and catch a train at Alchester; reach home by mid-morning, and tackle her prep — rather a ghastly prospect now; but with proper planning it could be done. Say two hours for each subject — eight hours' work. Bridie might come in and cook supper and make black coffee . . . but she didn't want to leave here yet. Like Guy and Lesley, she had fallen under the spell of the place, the old house with its lavender-coloured autumn garden, the golden grove and wild orchard.

Going back, she heard voices in the shed. Guy must have finished work too.

But it wasn't Guy. As she reached the door she saw an old man sitting on the box. Lesley leaned against the bench, her face turned towards him, looking so strange that Rowan almost called out in surprise. In fact she made no sound, but, as though feeling her reaction, Lesley looked across, saw her and exclaimed, "Rowan — something dreadful's happened."

"I can see. What *is* it?"

"Mr. Trussler's been telling me . . ." The old man was leaning forward on a stick, watching her. He had one of those intelligent otter-like English faces, slightly pug-nosed, with bright black eyes; but his expression was glum and stern.

Lesley held a typed paper in her fingers. She glanced at it, then back at the old man, still with that queer sick look.

Rowan waited. The garden door clapped open and shut — Guy was coming. He reached the shed door, stopped short as Rowan had done, and cried, "What's up?"

Lesley put the paper into his hand: "Go on — read that."

He took it, his eyes on her face. Then he began aloud: "'Gray Gavine. Plan for reclaiming wild garden. Starting date: Monday 19th October.'" He read more slowly. "'One: complete clearance all existing vegetation . . . weedkillers . . . roots . . . Bare earth and trees as framework. Two: all wild life to be exterminated. Three: replant with ground cover to prevent return of weeds . . .' What *is* this? A horror comic?"

No one spoke. He said, "Don't look like that. I thought there'd been a death at least."

"There soon will be," said Lesley. "A whole lot of deaths — it's all down there: 'Mice, shrews, hedgehogs, moles, grass snakes, water voles' — water voles, for God's sake! What harm are *they* supposed to do?"

He asked mildly, "But what's all the gloom about? It can't happen here. Mrs. Gray would never have it."

"Of course not! But she's not to know a thing until it's finished."

At that he did look startled. Lesley went on: "Some bright young man came here a couple of Sundays ago, just after she'd left for Paris. He wants to be a 'garden consultant' — or whatever they call it. A sort of Atrocity Brown, in his case. He saw the pré, and he's got Graham Gray to give him a free hand, to 'reclaim' it, if you please. And wait, guess what else? — it's to be a special present for Karen Gray, a glorious surprise when she gets home in the New Year. What do you think of that?"

"They're out of their minds." He turned to the old man. "Surely you told him —"

Lesley interposed, "Oh, Mr. Trussler didn't know a thing about it, nor did anyone else till this paper came into the office yesterday. All signed and sealed. Starting tomorrow week, bringing his own firing squad."

Guy looked staggered. Lesley quoted bitterly, "'Wild life to be exterminated' — Karen Gray will love that bit, won't she? She's never allowed any traps or shooting in the pré."

She went on meditatively, "Do you know how they kill moles nowadays? Father was telling me. None of those old springes, it's all scientific now. You gas them, wipe them out with cyanide, or you put down poisoned worms in the runs. Too many moles, too many rabbits and seals and foxes . . . there are too many *people*."

Rowan heard herself exclaim, "But it's been done to people!"

"But they've other people to speak up for them when they're dead, and say it was wrong. Moles die in agony underground and no one sees them and no one thinks it matters."

"I saw one yesterday. Alive. It was —" what was the word? Not pretty, certainly not playful-looking, like water voles or squirrels. Something about it had appealed to her, though; it was primitive, ferocious, and yet beautiful in a way: innocent. More like — yes: like an elephant seal. One didn't want it wiped out. She finished lamely, "It wasn't doing any harm."

"Still. We know about pests. That's the whole point of a place like this, they *aren't* doing any harm, they *needn't* be slaughtered. What fills me with despair is that sort of thing" — she pointed to the paper — "being turned out by someone setting up as an adviser, the very sort of creature who ought to know better." The old man made an impatient movement. ". . . Never giving a thought to what might be there already, just wading in with a flame gun, 'clearing the weeds'!"

Trussler spat: "Weeds! You just look what he reckons he's going to plant — all sorts of foreign muck. But Mr. Gray, you see, he wouldn't know the difference. Leaves it all to his mother. And this time of year — it would just look a mess, to him."

Guy said, "The idea was — to give this chap a start: was that it? His first commission. He'll learn, I suppose . . ."

"Learn! Not him."

"No," Lesley agreed. "He'll never learn anything. Wildlife's part of a garden — he ought to know that *first*. Butterflies and toads and hedgehogs. So he'd everything to gain by using a bit of heart and imagination and — and mercy," she finished almost inaudibly.

"Well, cheer up, darling — it's not going to happen here."

"Guy, who's going to stop it?"

"That's easy. You are. Karen would never forgive you if you didn't. So you'll tackle him tomorrow in London — Mr. Gray, I mean — get him to ask his mother first. That should do it."

"Do you think we hadn't thought of that! He's in New York. Angelo told me. They don't even know when he'll be back."

"All the better. So you can tell her yourself. You must." Rowan thought she could see the advantage of habitual silence. When Guy did talk he was impressive. Already looking less wretched, Lesley began thinking aloud:

"Telephone? Write? I suppose I can wire. Rather a mouthful though . . ."

Guy said quietly, "I think it's far too urgent for that. Go and see her."

"What?"

"Yes. Where is she, Portugal? They'll know at the house."

"Oh, I've got her address, she wrote about the bulbs. No, the thing is — she's still in Paris."

"Then that's fine. Send her word tonight, fly over tomorrow." He picked up Tray, who caught the rising breeze of optimism and began to purr.

Lesley sat still. They all looked at her. She said in a dazed way, "Yes, but — I must take Tabby. We'd have to stay. Fifty pounds? A hundred? I haven't got it."

"Don't be silly, I have."

"And my job . . ."

"Tell them you must have three days off. You can get another job. But the pré — if it goes, it goes. You'd never see it back in your lifetime."

"No. But —"

"The money? Oh, leave it to me in your will! On second thoughts," he said, "why don't I come too? I'll fix it, shall I? We'll all go."

"Oh yes! But," smiling, "if you go, I needn't?"

"No, no, you're the gardener, you must tell the tale. Unless you'd rather Mr. Trussler . . . ?"

The old fellow produced an arch grin and left them to it. Guy and Lesley strolled away towards the car, laughing and making their plans.

Rowan stayed for a minute longer, looking back from the door.

Gardening wasn't the answer for herself; but she was glad they had brought her. This was a place to return to.

The sun was gone. The wild place was deep in shadow now, chill with dew and with approaching winter. Reclaimed, though: there would be spring, and here it would still be. She could come and see it. She imagined thin roots, snowdrops and crocuses, stirring already in the ancient turf, under the straggle of October weeds; the growth that had sheltered primrose, violet, cowslip through the summer.

What was it people had said to one as a child? — *It won't run away.* You couldn't say that so glibly now, but sometimes it would still be true. Before the destroyer moved in there would be the chance of the miracle, the last-minute reprieve, one more spring.

CHAPTER
SIXTEEN

Rowan woke with a jump when a bird fell on to her pillow. Confused perhaps by some chance reflection it dashed through the open window, soared, struck the ceiling, crashed and lay still. Dead? It was small, slender, silvery-blue; a nuthatch? She took it in her hand. It lay limp. She breathed into the pathetic gaping beak. A white eyelid moved, an eye met hers in wild surmise; the heart fluttered, plunged and throbbed steadily. She held her hand to the window. The nuthatch bit her finger sharply and flew.

Five minutes later she closed the cottage door behind her. It was light, the air filled with pink and yellow sunrise. No sound came from the bodyguards sprawled in the estate car. She tiptoed past.

On the open hill a keen wind blew from the sea. She felt strangely light and happy, running down-wind; "free as a bird". It struck her that she had outgrown that hopeless love; in the past few days she had found herself, struggled clear of some chrysalis. For years she had felt trapped, tied down, a victim, like a person caught by witchcraft. She remembered the message she had sent Hicks: the snare was broken, she was escaped.

And — she realized — all through this time in the country, people had talked to her, and had gone on talking; and quite often she had known what to answer, or even what not to answer. That had never happened before. Was she going to be all right, after all?

She looked up. Someone was about in the plantations. She could hear whistling. A man appeared at the stile, vaulted it — a young man, then. He approached, whistling away. No one she knew. Yet when he saw her he broke off, waved and called, "Hello. Off already?" Just as though he knew who she was and where she was going. Odd. She stood still. Coming nearer, he added, "Glad I was early."

He was slight, fresh-faced, with light curly hair — no, she was sure she'd never seen him before. Yet he did remind her of someone. There had been so many new people — it would come to her in a minute.

He seemed in no doubt about her. "You're Ralph's cousin — Ralph Oliver? Got something here for him." He was opening a rucksack, taking out a square package wrapped in stiff new brown paper, secured with good string. He stood weighing it in his hand, smiling at her.

Something for Ralph? He went on in that easy tone, sure of himself and yet diffident too — "I just thought I'd bring it along. I knew Ralph years ago."

She took the parcel. It had hard outlines, like a box, inside some kind of wrapping.

"What is it?"

"Well — it's rather funny. Remember the storm a few weeks back — the 21st September — that high wind?"

257

She nodded. A sycamore had blown down at Nine Wells.

He went on slowly, "We lost a good many trees in Sussex. One was — an old chestnut, on my father's place. He's a head forester."

She looked at him, waiting.

"An old hollow tree. When they cleared it up they found all sorts — bits of metal from a Jerry plane that came down in the war. And inside — birds' nests, squirrels' nests, the lot. But right at the top —"

"*Oh!*"

"This. A sort of hoard. An old satchel it looks like, black mouldy, and a tin box inside, all rusted up. Dad unwrapped it and had a look, and there's something with Ralph's name. An old book, I think he said — and an address, somewhere in Ireland."

She couldn't speak.

"Always climbing, wasn't he?" The young man laughed. "No, of course, you wouldn't remember. Well, I thought he might like to have a look at it one day, for a bit of fun."

"Yes . . . I expect . . . *yes.*"

"We asked around — it didn't seem the sort of thing to send off to Ireland, out of the blue, even if he still lives there. So I meant to write to that television place, some time. And then you ran into my uncle! I'd told him about Dad finding the stuff. So I thought you'd take it back with you. That all right?"

"Yes. Only — your uncle?" Where had she met *him*? At the parish meeting, the shop, the Fox and Hounds?

"My uncle in the police."

"Sergeant Lamb!"

"That's the one."

She remembered Sergeant Lamb's notebook. And then, in a flash of memory — "Oh, wait! You're — you must be — Tim Lamb! Are you? The boy that could sing?"

He looked astonished: pleased as well. "Now how could you possibly know that?"

"My aunt told me. You went to school with Ralph. That school in the forest?"

They stood and looked at one another. Her head was buzzing with questions. She couldn't ask them yet — but she might never have another chance. She said in anguish, "Oh, I have to go."

He turned, they were walking together, getting over the stile, going down through the misty thickets to the road. In a dream she heard him say, "You'll be down again? I work around here myself. Forestry commission. See you, then."

He was gone; but it was all right. They were going to meet again. She stumbled down the hill, bemused, clasping the parcel. It was breathtaking, full of promise. A voice from the past, embodied in — what relics? This hoard must have been hidden long ago, before the war. It might hold anything — the stuffed squirrel, even the long-lost owl whistle. She must get home quickly and open it. Why not here? No, it was too valuable to be pulled apart, haphazard.

And then, beginning to run, she realized that her thoughts of freedom had been an illusion. The old spell

259

was there, as strong as ever. It would go on, it would never let her go. And nothing would come of it.

Nothing? That was absurd too. She thought of *Villette*, that chart of secret unrequited love, "such perhaps as many a human being passes through life without ever knowing". One couldn't call that nothing. Perhaps it was life itself, quest, adventure, fate — how could one know? Not yet, not yet.

> *Love without hope, as when the young bird-*
> *catcher*
> *Swept off his tall hat to the Squire's own*
> *daughter,*
> *So let the imprisoned larks escape to fly*
> *Singing about her head, as she rode by.*

At the Woodman no one was stirring. She found her bicycle, strapped the package in the saddlebag and started along the lane. The sky was bright, the wind streaming with grey clouds, brown leaves, white thistledown. Rowan trees, fawn and silver, were blowing in the dark yew woods. A string of racehorses appeared, coming down the bridle path from the gallops. She braked, put one foot to the ground and waited for them to cross the road.

They had passed, and she did not move. She was staring after them — not at the horses now, but the riders, the stable lads; all alike in breeches and thick jerseys, but —

"But they were girls," she whispered half aloud. "Three of them — they were *girls*."

The yard doors were shutting. Behind them now she could hear the familiar sounds going on, horses moving, neighing, whickering, sneezing; and girls' voices, girls running to and fro, busy and dedicated, doing the job she could do, the things she had been learning all her life. No need to wonder about the future: it wouldn't run away. It was here; or in some other stable. Not just at Nine Wells. The world was full of stables — why had that never struck her before? It would be waiting, the only life she ever wanted: her job in the country.

Overhead the wind vane swayed and flashed, the bright racehorse pointed west. She flew on.